Magical
Mechanications

MAGICAL MECHANICATIONS

PIP BALLANTINE & TEE MORRIS

Imagine That!
STUDIOS

www.ministryofpeculiaroccurrences.com

For Katie

❖⇒◦⇐❖

The other daughter we never had

The older sister you didn't expect to be

An inspiration to your American family

Always

Other Books
from
Pip Ballantine & Tee Morris

THE MINISTRY OF PECULIAR OCCURRENCES

VERITY FITZROY & THE MINISTRY SEVEN

Mechanical Wings

PIP BALLANTINE

Eleanor stood in the shadow of her father, and watched him slip the golden ring on the finger of the wickedest person in any of the floating cities. Her protestations, her scream of outrage lay still on her tongue like a painful stone. One that she would have gladly spat out into the world—but dared not.

Faine Escrew was tall, beautiful and the richest woman in all of the sky. She also had a heart as dark as a moonless, starless night, and not an ounce of pity for any living creature in her blood. As she turned and looked over her shoulder at Eleanor and her brothers standing on the steps of the palace below her, a smile lingered on her lips. It was one that some might have said was beautiful, but the princess knew was more of a smirk than anything else.

King Ivan had long ago passed into Faine's iron grip—anything that Eleanor said now would be wasted on him. However, her brothers were not so circumspect. Iain, the youngest of the King's sons, and of the eleven the closest to his sister in age but furthest in temperament, could not keep his words to himself.

"Snake," he whispered under his breath, his blue eyes narrowed in hatred. Too late Eleanor shot him a look to silence him. A slight shift in Faine's back told that she had heard Iain's comment.

All unaware the aristocracy and common folk of the City of Swans, watched their monarch marry his second wife. Perhaps they hoped he would not have quite so many children with this one, but more likely no thoughts at all occupied their minds. Madame Escrew had that effect on people. The dirigible city relied on her trade for its mere existence.

Every ship in this city, tethered one to another, filled the envelopes of their airships with gas mined from her mountain estate. Those ships that could not afford the precious æther from the Escrew Conglomerate, would eventually be cut loose from the city as a whole, and be allowed to drift downwards into the boiling earth beneath the clouds.

It was a fair enough reason not to stand against her, but it didn't make it any easier for Princess Eleanor.

Furthest down the stairs stood Eric and Merion, the eldest of her brothers. They were whispering to one another, not bothering to even try to be covert. She had eleven brothers, and all of them were far too rash.

Finally, the ceremony was over, and the priest proclaimed them husband and wife. As the crowd cheered—somewhat weakly Eleanor thought—the couple retired into the bowels of the cathedral ship to begin the arcane right of crowning Madame Escrew queen.

Eleanor released an angry sigh, spun around, and walked down the steps towards the knot of princes waiting for her.

Eleven brothers. The other Cities, particularly Eagle and Owl, were jealous of the surplus of sons the King of Swan City possessed. Eleanor could tell them it was not everything that they imagined, especially for a lone princess. Much as she loved her brothers, sometimes it felt like she was floating in a sky full of men. At times like this in fact.

Instead of complaining, she led the way back to the palace with not a comment to her brothers except for a curt look. They fell into step around her, all varying shades of blond and brown hair. Just like that her feelings towards her brothers changed. Instead of swallowing her this phalanx of tall men were providing comfort. Now, they were her own personal army.

She knew full well, that was what Madame Escrew feared.

On reaching the palace, Eleanor ignored the throne room, drawing them all up to their study. It was here they learned of the history of the City of Swans, mathematics, geography, and navigation. Here and now, Eleanor would be the teacher, her brothers dutiful students.

Eric, the eldest at nearly thirty sat himself on the window, and peered into the swirling clouds below. The palace ship was in the centre of the city, but gaps between the ships meant that the reality of their existence could still be seen. "That woman—" he began, but his sister held up her hand.

Eleanor pinned up the long curls of dark hair into a far more utilitarian bun than the court fashion she'd worn to the wedding. Then, she darted to her desk and withdrew the dragonflies she had spent the last week working on. This had been done out of the sight of Madame Escrew naturally. While the brothers watched, she carefully wound up the five gleaming machines with the two tiny keys in their abdomens before releasing them. With a flicker of bright green, they leapt into the air and began to circle the room in a cloud.

They darted about from ceiling to floor. They had only been airborne for mere moments when one quickly grabbed something hidden on top of the bookshelf. The brothers all winced as a high-pitched whine echoed through the library, which was about as enjoyable as fingernails scratched down a blackboard.

The little gleaming predator pulled loose a long whip like creature not much longer than it was. As the brothers watched wide-eyed, the dragonfly ripped it apart with its gleaming articulated legs. Eleanor smiled, but she waited until her creations had circled the rest of the library.

"We should be safe to speak freely now," she said, arranging her ridiculous dress as she sat on a stool.

"Eleanor," Alan whispered, his eyes following the continuing path of the machines as they buzzed around the room, "they are incredible. I didn't know you could build such marvellous things."

Their sister shrugged. "Neither did I truth be known, brother. Something about that woman's presence in the palace just brings out the inventiveness in me. I remember seeing a plan of them in one of those books that old tinker showed us last summer."

"Finally that memory of yours is some use," Roger, who had been her childhood competitor, flicked a balled up piece of paper on the desk at her.

"Madame Escrew might take you as her apprentice," Maximilian laughed.

Eleanor felt something like a hard sob form in her belly. Once they had been genuinely merrier. This very room had rung with laughter and learning.

"I blame myself," she whispered, even as she held out her hand for one of the dragonflies to return to her. "After Mother's death I should have taken better care of Father. I should have noticed he was so lonely. Madame Escrew would never have—"

"It's not your fault, Ellie." Alan grasped her hand. "We were all distraught when it happened. None of us ever thought…"

"No, we did not!" She snapped, yanking her arm free and turning away before they could see her tears. "That is what she counted on. She saw an opportunity and she took it. Now we must deal with the consequences."

Out the window, their flag of a rampant swan fluttered in the always-constant breeze, seeming to challenge her.

"What can we do?" Alan went relentlessly on. "Father is utterly bewitched by her."

"We must find a way," she said with determination. "Not just for ourselves, but for the city itself. We must be like her, and find an opportunity."

The siblings looked on her, the silence as thick as the tension of the day. One by one, they retired to their rooms, choosing to miss on the revels of the evening and avoid the new queen.

The next morning, Eleanor forwent any assistance by her maid and dressed herself. The princess went down to breakfast on the very edge of being late. The less time she had to spend in her new stepmother's presence the better. Apparently her brothers had either been down early, or had abandoned any thought of food whatsoever because she was alone with her father and his queen.

The three of them sat at the long table, while being served by masked servants. They served grilled flying fish, starling eggs, and expensive grilled bacon to the silent royals.

It was the new Queen that broke the stillness. Her voice like silk. "You are looking very pale, Eleanor. Are you well?"

"Not at all, thank you," the princess replied, concentrating on the food before her. She stabbed an egg with a certain misplaced anger.

"It is just this is the season for insects, and I would hate to think you have been bitten by something…nasty." Madame's hard brown eyes locked with Eleanor's just as determined blue ones. The princess did not need to be told; the new queen had noticed her listening device in the library had been removed.

"What could be nasty in our palace?" Eleanor said mildly. "All is so wonderful here. If any such vermin were to infest our hallowed halls, Your Majesty, I would take action. Have no fear."

Eleanor's eyes flicked over to King Ivan, who remained oblivious to their verbal sparring. He was nothing like the man he had been before his real Queen's death.

Madame Escrew tilted her head and smiled a smile like an iron barb. "Indeed, the palace is a wonderful place to grow up, but still…" She paused and placed her hand over the King's. "Even a princess should have a use. Don't you think, my love? It does not set a good example for the citizens to have your daughter seen idle around the palace." Faine leaned over and placed a kiss on the King's cheek. "Too long have your children frittered away their time without a mother's touch."

Eleanor's cheeks flamed red at the suggestion that she was idle and that Madame was anything like a mother. "Reading is not being idle. It is feeding the mind."

King Ivan jerked upright as if he'd been struck, and stared at his daughter as if seeing her for the first time; and Eleanor flinched. She had never seen her father look at her in that way.

"Yes," he rasped, "everything and everyone must have a purpose in the City of Swans."

Eleanor swallowed hard, feeling tears spring in the corner of her eyes.

She watched her stepmother rise, fighting the urge to pull free of her touch when she snatched up one of her hands, flipping it over as if it were a dead frog. "Look at that; as soft as cheese! By your age, my dear, my hands were scarred and toughened by tightening screws, and forging parts for my father's machines."

The King nodded mechanically. "It would be good for Eleanor to see the other side of privilege."

"Yes, not all of your subjects can write with diamond pencils on golden slates," Faine said, her eyes still fixed on her as she returned to the King's side.

Her father grinned like an idiot, and pushed back from the table to stare at her. "What do you suggest then my darling? How can we make Eleanor aware how truly blessed she is?"

Madame scraped up the last of her bacon and starling eggs, dispatching it with neat efficiency. "My engineer Stella would make an excellent teacher for the princess. Some call her a witch, and it is true she has many secrets that should not die with her. She is, after all, old. Quite frail."

Eleanor's calm shattered as she leapt to her feet, knocking her chair over in the process. "Father!" she protested. "I refused to be judged by this woman. Surely you can't mean to send me away? What have I ever done to deserve being used so ill?"

Thunder clouds gathered in her father's gaze; a darkness that she had never seen there before. Plenty of grief she'd seen in his eyes, but always lightened by his love for his children. He was a stranger to her in that moment.

"Done?" he growled. "Done, my daughter? You have done nothing! That is precisely the point. You will do as your Mother suggests, and be grateful for the chance to improve yourself."

She knew a pointless fight when she saw one before her. "At least let me say goodbye to my brothers," she whispered, dropping her head.

"They are busy with their own work," the King muttered, as he slurped down some tea.

Eleanor clenched her jaw shut hard. As she had grown older, her father had become a benevolent, if distant, figure. She had always been able to dream that he loved her in some kind of way. All through the brief courtship of Madame Escrew and the King, Eleanor had felt even that tenuous connection disappearing. In this particular moment, hard and brutal as it was she realized that it was completely gone.

Now there was only the hope of salvaging the remains of her family and the rest of the City.

So she smiled in what she hoped was the manner of an obedient child and tilted her head. "Then I look forward to being of some use to you Father. And will attend Miss Stella and learn what I can."

A bitter bile welled in her throat. Anyone remotely connected with Madame Escrew was not someone she wanted to meet.

leanor barely had a chance to wipe her mouth on the linen napkin before Madame was leading her to the door. A footman was waiting under the arch of the Great Hall, a small traveling case and an abashed expression across his own face.

"Please do give sweet Stella my regards," Madame said, her voice full of false delight. The feeling of her hand pressed into the small of the princess' back was like a hovering knife. It made Eleanor think of her own desires the previous day, and wish again for a blade of her own.

No, Eleanor decided, *I will have to wait a little while. Find out her secrets and a way behind all her defences.*

Eleanor looked to her father, one last time, but saw there was nothing to be had there. His eyes were elsewhere. He did not even bother to wave her off.

As she was escorted down the stairs, out the door of the palace, and towards the city dock, Eleanor's throat tightened. Maybe she hadn't expected to be allowed to see her brothers, but she might have hoped one might come down the stairs by chance. With eleven of them there was a decent statistical possibility...

Nothing.

She shot a glance back at the gleaming spires of the palace, and a fear grew in her. Had Madame done something to them? Were they already dead?

No, the princess reminded herself, *Madame might be able to bend Father's will on me, but his sons—my brothers—are another matter.*

The ferry that waited for her was piloted by a grey-faced old man, with one eye replaced by a battered onyx stone. She did not know him by sight but saw immediately by his expression that he would be no friend to her. Madame's minions had been infiltrating all levels of the kingdom for quite some time now.

Silently, Eleanor took up a place at the prow of the airship, setting her eyes to the horizon of gleaming silver clouds. The ferry pulled away from the City of Swans, and she swallowed hard on the realization that this was the first time she'd been away from the place of her birth. She'd previously dreamed of adventure beyond the safety of her father's kingdom; it was cruel irony that she was achieving her dreams at the hands of her enemy.

The ferry was old but not as slow as she wished it was. With the engines chugging and guided by the morose captain, they pulled quickly away from the city and found a fair current. It was as if nature herself was against the princess. By the evening Eleanor no longer had the comfort of ignorance in her destination.

They were turning towards the distant crags where Madame held sway, and with every mile Eleanor could feel her stomach clench in an unhappy knot. The surface was a place no city dweller wanted to think of; contaminated, dangerous, where your body was consigned to when you died, and a place no sensible citizen would ever travel to. However, it did provide some resources that were necessary to their lives.

The princess walked reluctantly to the prow of the ferry and watched the destination resolve itself before her. Ahead the grey tips of the mountains were now becoming visible, rising out of the clouds like thick knuckles. As they drew even nearer she could make out square buildings dotted over their surface, accompanied by chimney stacks billowing smoke out into the winds.

It was not a scene to inspire confidence. By the time the ferry pulled next to the dock and tied up, Eleanor's nostrils were full of the choking sulphurous door Madame's industry created. The bleak grey rock, harboured no life, and the buildings had few windows to greet her. It was as far removed from the City of Swans as it was possible to get. It felt as though she had travelled for days to get here, and she was cut off from everything—including the love of her brothers.

It would be exactly what Madame Escrew had planned from the beginning. At that thought Eleanor straightened her back. She had to remember her royal heritage. She had to remember every detail of her trials so she could draw on it for strength in the battle yet to come. That memory of hers would be useful once more.

A tall, burly man, dressed in dusty grey clothing, and covered by a leather apron stood waiting for her. His eyes were as welcoming as the stone beneath their feet. The effect was only enhanced by the fact that he wore a filtering mask that completely covered the lower half of his face. He could have been grinning or leering beneath it, and she would never know. "Come," he muttered, jerking his head, and turning away.

Eleanor contemplated what might happen should she refuse his curt command but decided this was a fight not quite worth fighting. Instead, she followed in his wake, past rumbling factories, and ranks of dead-eyed men filing in and out of them. As she went she held her sleeve over her mouth and tried not to choke.

Finally, they reached a building with a large door with a mechanical wheel attached to it that was nearly as tall as Eleanor herself. Her nameless guide spun the wheel with some little effort and pulled the door open. The shriek it gave would have made the dead flinch. Without waiting to be asked Eleanor stepped inside.

It was as she expected. Her guide slammed the door and spun the wheel behind her back. With a concentration of will the princess did not flinch, but instead carefully examined her surroundings. Since the interior of the building was illuminated only by half a dozen dim lanterns attached to the walls, it was made that much harder.

She was able to make out ten long benches laid out and at the far end of the cavernous space a forge with all the tools necessary for casting metals. She and her brother Brian had shared an interest in metal work, and curious despite the situation, Eleanor stepped further into the workroom. She ran her fingers lightly over the items she could now make out laid out on the benches.

Automatons in various shapes and forms were easy to identify. They covered half the work space, while the other benches had cogs, gears, pistons, and pieces of boilers laid out in patterns she could not comprehend. She paused to examine them, her brow furrowed.

Automatons were becoming popular in the City of Swans, but they were still restricted to simple tasks; pouring tea, answering doorbells, and perhaps walking the dog. As her fingers traced over the inner workings, she began to perceive that whoever the maker of this was, they had managed to miniaturize so many of the parts that these figures when finished could take on far more varied activities.

"Interesting way of saying hello you have—rummaging around in my work!" The voice that came out of the shadows was so sharp and unexpected that Eleanor dropped the fly-wheel she'd been examining with a clatter. The figure that emerged from the rear of the workspace was as incredible as the works in progress on the benches.

Eleanor quite forgot her manners and stared. The woman was small and old, her grey hair tangled and matted as if she had little care for it. It was however only on one half of her head. The other portion was a construction of naked gears and cogs that approximated the remaining part of her skull. Her right eye was a bleary cataract covered blue mortal eye while the other was a gleaming gem that must have been the largest diamond that Eleanor had ever seen. The strangeness was not limited to her face, for whatever traumatic event had stolen it, had also taken much of her body too. The whole right side of her body was a collection of gleaming brass. An articulated hand was wrapped around a wrench, and when the woman moved forward it was with a pronounced limp. Beneath the leather metal-worker's apron Eleanor knew there would be more wonders to behold. This then was the witch Madame had spoken of.

The princess swallowed hard and waved her arm to take in the work laid out. "I couldn't help myself, this is so fascinating. I do a little tinkering myself, but this…"

The woman's snort was an odd concoction of human and mechanical sounds; the wheezing of lungs along with the sound of air striking metal.

Eleanor cleared her throat and dared to venture, "Stella?"

Eyes, both flesh and jewelled focused on her. "Indeed. I am guessing She sent you."

Eleanor had no way of knowing how deep the clouds she was stepping out into where, so the princess kept her tone moderate. "Yes, the new Queen. She told me you were a friend of hers…"

Stella lurched forward, throwing her weight unexpectedly towards Eleanor. She managed not to yell in shock, or to move—but it wouldn't have made any difference. A long chain, gleaming in the faint light, pulled the woman up short. It was attached the good human leg she still had.

"Made it myself," she said with a bleak grin. "She challenged me to make a device even I could not break. And I—in my arrogance did." She rattled it once more. "Forged the steel with my own blood. Hard magic to break that. I suppose I could saw my damn leg off, but…" she paused and shook her head. "I haven't quite reached that point. Haven't got much humanity left as it is."

The princess nodded, not quite knowing how to reply to that. In the end, she said nothing. It must have been the right thing to do as Stella, once the greatest tinker to be found in any City, took Eleanor princess of the Swans into her apprenticeship.

Unlike the older woman she was not chained, but the door was locked securely, and only the faceless guard came to deliver food twice a day. They were a pair of prisoners.

Soon enough Eleanor forgot all about that. In her father's palace she had toyed with mechanics and engineering, but under Stella's tutelage she was given total focus. Her new teacher would tolerate no idle moments, not even thinking of anything else. Nor was she shy about punishment. She would leave tools hot, or sharp edges bared so that the princess would burn or cut herself.

Soon enough, Eleanor learned to observe where everything lay in the workshop. She also learned the fine art of cogs, wheels, pistons, boilers, and the little magics used to bring them to the peak of their abilities. Stella, she soon discovered, was a mistress of weaving, not just metals together, but also the magic of blood and flesh. It was this that made her prosthetics possible and would in time bring the automatons to life.

Eleanor would have thought the rough, sometimes verging on cruel treatment she received from Stella would have driven her mad, but the truth of it was, she was learning in addition to the witch's art, something of the witch herself.

Once, when Stella was fitting a fly wheel into the housing of the most complete automaton, she caught a proud smile on her fellow captive's face. Eleanor however knew she was losing herself in the endless progress of days. She had lost count, and been so immersed in the interesting work that she'd not thought to keep a tally.

One morning—though she could not have identified which one—they sat, on each side of the door eating their cold breakfast in silence, and the princess realized it was a different silence. Instead of being awkward and painful, the quiet was companionable. Somewhere in the uncounted days they had reached an accord.

The question remained if she could spin it out into something more than that.

Cautiously, Eleanor began to speak. She drew her finger through the dust on the floor. "I confess I wonder what is happening in the outside world." She did not mention her brothers or the City of Swans, but she had to lower her head least Stella see her thoughts in her expression.

Instead of speaking, the witch climbed to her feet, and tugged her chain after her to the window. It was small, shuttered and usually never opened, but Stella unhooked the latch and pushed the coverings aside. Moonlight flooded in, and Eleanor recognized with a start that it was night beyond the walls of their prison. She didn't want to see the outside world—even if it was the stained, bleak world of the rock—but Stella gestured her over.

Together then, they peered out into the night. The sulphurous clouds were still there, but a breeze was wafting them back and forward in front of the full moon. Eleanor felt a knot of sadness choke her throat, and would have turned away to the harsh reality of their work, when Stella grabbed her arm and pulled her back. "Look!" she rasped.

The princess stepped back and turned her gaze to where the witch was pointing. She saw shadows against the moon. They were more solid than clouds and shaped like great birds. Eleanor shook her head, and with a frown tried harder to discern what they were. They could not be owls, for the City of Owls had been breached and sunk over a hundred years ago—and besides these shapes were far too big.

They had long slender necks and huge wings. They were swans!

"What swans would fly at night?" she wondered out loud.

"Watch," Stella whispered, her rancid breath hot against Eleanor's cheek.

The group of swans turned in the moonlight, and the princess gasped. These were no creatures of feather and flesh. The light caught them and gleamed on brass and iron, etching each metallic feather in a gleam of white. The long articulated necks flexed beautifully with each downward beat. Eleanor was entranced at this display of the maker's art. The artistry of the work burned into her memory.

"They are amazing," she stammered, pressing her fingertips against the glass as though she could somehow reach through and touch them.

"Yes, they are," the witch replied, "but you are only seeing skin deep. Do you not see how many there are?"

Eleanor didn't understand, but she did as she was bidden. Her gaze flickered over the slowly moving group. "Ten...eleven..." She stopped immediately that the words were out of her mouth.

"Eleven birds. Eleven brothers," Stella breathed into the ear of the princess.

"No!" Eleanor flicked her head and stared at the witch. "She can't have—"

"As clever as we are in this day and age, there are some things that even the greatest tinker cannot do better than a living being." Stella looked out the window again, following the circling flight of the mechanical birds. "Sometimes a sacrifice is required."

"My brothers..." Eleanor whispered, thinking of them all; some more beloved than others, but all dear to her. They were her blood.

"Now they are Her creatures," Stella returned. "They will be absorbed into the machine and eventually become part of it."

Eleanor's mind was spinning, but she watched her brothers for a moment until it came it to her. "Eventually?" She grabbed hold of Stella. "You mean they are not already?"

The witch shook her head, her brass jaw working, but sagged in the other woman's grasp. Finally, she ground out, "No, not yet. It will take a month for the transformation to be complete, and the machine to take all of their humanity beyond the ability to get them out alive."

"Then there is a chance?"

Even Stella's jewelled eye could not meet Eleanor's, but she finally did manage to grunt out, "Yes."

So there it was. Eleanor sat back and thought for a moment. She thought about how she'd always had to be the sensible one, and how her brothers had always come to her for advice, because princes were supposed to know everything. She thought about how—trapped as they were now in their mechanical swan bodies—they would most definitely want her advice, and yet for once she had to ask someone else for it.

Carefully, she cleared her throat, and probed Stella further, "So, how would I go about getting my brothers back?"

The witch stepped away from the window, and dragged her chain clanking behind her back to the workbench. She jerked a magnifying glass down on a boom arm, adjusted the gaslight brighter, and began to screw a tiny fly-wheel into the chest of the automaton—all the time as though nothing had happened.

Eleanor could hardly believe it; after all it was Stella that had showed her the scene out the window in the first place. She walked over to the witch and stood behind her shoulder, silent and waiting. She was completely at a loss to know what words to use that would get Stella to help her. Perhaps the witch had only wanted to drag her fellow captive down into the mire of despair she had been in for so long.

It appeared that silence weighed on Stella, because after a moment, she sighed heavily and put down the screwdriver. "To break the magic and undo the machines you would need to make skins for them."

"Skins?"

"Her magic and tinkering are strongest when creating creatures for the air, and you would need to counter that by building metallic vices to interfere with her workings. It is the only way to allow the men to come out of the machines."

"How do you know about my brothers?"

"I've always known who you are," Stella tilted her head. "She talked about you a great deal. Well, you, your brothers and your father. I don't know why..." The witch's voice trailed off as though she were thinking on something unpalatable.

Eleanor shuddered, however she was not going to travel old paths with her fellow prisoner. She had to think of the future.

"So, I can make the cloaks here, and we can save them?"

Stella flinched, presumably at the liberal use of the word 'we'. "Even if I wanted to help you, I don't have the necessities here. Spun silver must be used to make the cloaks—it is the only material that can bear the magical component."

"Silver?" Eleanor bit her lip. "The City of Eagles is the only place to get quantities of that."

Stella croaked out a laugh. "Even Madame dares not attack that city—at least not yet. There is more and worse to hear." She rubbed her finger on the rough edge of the nearby hacksaw.

Her pregnant pause drove Eleanor crazy, but she managed not to snap.

"It is the silence you see." Stella smirked, and for a second the princess worried that she could read her thoughts. "You have to bind a bit of your soul into each cloak, and every ounce of your being must be bent to the task. Every sinew and effort must be put into this undertaking. Should you speak you would destroy not only the materials but the magic too." The witch shot her a gaze out of the corner of one eye.

"Silent the whole time?" Eleanor couldn't help an edge of dismay creeping into her voice. She could never remember having been silent for a day, let alone a month!

The other woman snorted. "You shouldn't have had so many brothers, should you!"

Eleanor frowned. "It wasn't as though I had a choice!"

Stella wanted to end the conversation there, but the princess would not be turned aside.

The next few days were spent trying to convince her fellow prisoner that they had to do this. The witch kept to her task of creating the automatons, but the princess could detect a change in her speed—as though other thoughts were tangling her concentration.

So, Eleanor kept lightly on, discussing how much of a challenge making the mechanical cloaks would be, and how the person who would do it would have to be a master of the craft. She even sketched out from memory the workings she had observed on the surface of the mechanical swans.

Stella grumbled, "Don't even try and tempt me, girl!" Yet she could not hide the light of interest in her eyes.

Eventually, on the third day after she had pointed out the swans to the princess, Stella set down the gruel she had been eating, and grabbed Eleanor's hand once more.

"If it is to be done, we must make our escape quickly. We will need every day that remains. If it can be done tonight then it should be."

Eleanor blinked. "What about you? This chain is not going to stretch all the way to the City of Eagles!"

Stella stared down blankly at the finely constructed chain. "She imprisoned me here with my own work, but it is held together by her magic. She said I did not know the meaning of loyalty and friendship, but I would know the strength of my failings. It is unbreakable."

"Unbreakable? There is no such thing," Eleanor said with the firmness of one who had studied every book on metallurgy she could find from an early age. She dropped to the floor and picked up the chain. It was heavy, and she observed spots on Stella's good leg were it had rubbed for years. As she studied the chain, she realized that it was in fact made up of several strands of metal, bound together tight, and that each was engraved with words. After fetching oculars and pliers from the workbench, she was able to read them. *Proud. Arrogant. Friendless.*

The strands labelled *Proud* and *Arrogant* were strong and seamless. She pulled and tugged at them fruitlessly with the pair of pliers. Nothing. However, when she applied the pliers to *Friendless* she felt it give a little.

With a grunt she was able to bend one strand. So the weakness was in the strand that was inscribed *Friendless*. The princess stared through the magnifying glass at the hairs-width crack and then glanced up at Stella.

"It's hopeless isn't it," the witch muttered, and since they had spent so much time together, Eleanor was able to discern that the bleak disinterest her fellow captive had been wrapped in when she arrived, was nothing more than an act now.

She managed to smother a smile, but dared to pat the witch's leg. "I am not leaving without you. We need each other."

Stella swallowed, but when the princess bent once more she saw that the strand now looked corroded. Now when she applied the pliers and tugged, the strand snapped.

"Holy steam!" Stella yelped.

One strand was all it took—even the remaining two could not hold themselves together without the third. While the witch watched, the princess pulled the chain rope apart and gently untwined it from her leg.

Stella stared at it a moment, her breathing unsteady. "I could have cut off my own leg," she muttered, "but she knew I would never do that."

"Now you don't have to," Eleanor whispered.

The witch's lips twisted, and her eye glittered dangerously. "She also thought me too far gone. Lost to humanity. She never was very good at judging kindness in people. It is a quality she knows little about."

The two women clasped hands tight.

"Then I think we should go and teach her how wrong she is," Eleanor said with a savage grin. "What do we need to proceed?"

"I'll show you."

Together then, they raced around the workshop, taking the specialized tools that Stella pointed out, and shoving them into a pair of large canvas bags. They took the sketches that the princess had made, and she saw with some pride that the witch had made some notations on them already while she hadn't been looking. The last item that Stella insisted on was a jar of gleaming gems; tiny pinpricks of light that looked like trapped fireflies. "Starlight opals," Stella said with a grin. "We will need these for the cloaks."

Eleanor knew that a combination of tinkering and magic would be required, but starlight opals were the rarest stones to be found in the cloud mountains. That the witch had so many was heart stopping.

Yet, neither of them could afford to stop for anything. Stella picked up a mallet and tossed Eleanor a thick metal spike. It passed briefly through her mind that only a few weeks ago, she would not have had the strength and dexterity to catch it so easily. Yet she did.

Placing the spike on the bottom hinge, she glanced at the witch. She did not flinch when Stella struck it hard. The hinges broke away like children's candy, and the door fell out with a muffled bang.

The chill night air invaded the princess' chest and she gasped reflexively. Suddenly the task of freeing her brothers lay before her. Yet, she paused for a moment, letting her eyes adjust to the weak moonlight. Thankfully at night, the factories ran on reduced workers, and the clouds of poisonous smoke were lessened. Both woman pulled the front of their shirts up over the mouths.

"The ferry," Stella hissed. "It is the only airship we can manage, with just the two of us."

Eleanor nodded. It looked quiet out there, and the ferry was not far. If they unhitched it and floated away, they could start the engine once they were clear of the mountain.

So the two of them scuttled in the shadows of the factories, towards the ships. The whole place was so still that Eleanor could hear her heartbeat in her head, but their footfalls were softened by the thick layers of ash, and they made it to the pier with no signs of pursuit. Quickly as they dared, they unhitched the ferry.

Eleanor began to breathe again—or at least it felt to her like she did. She had just slipped onto the deck from the dock, when a group of men stepped down from a larger airship on the other side. For an instant, the women and the men stared at each other in the moonlight. Then the men snatched up their rifles. Eleanor standing exposed on the deck, made a perfect target, but when the rifles of Madame's soldiers came about, it was Stella that stepped before them.

Eleanor screamed, but the weapons fired anyway. The witch fell, but the soldiers had one more barrel to unleash, and they turned again on the princess.

That was when her own art—almost forgotten—saved her. A cloud of gleaming green shapes darted down. They were sharp and metallic, and glowed in the dusky confusion of the clouds. Eleanor recognized the shapes—her little mechanical dragonflies that she'd made back in the palace.

Yet these little creations of the tinker's art did not come to their creator. The dragonflies, with their sharp, long legs flew at the soldiers—straight for their eyes. It was the last thing they could have expected, and they actually shouted in surprise.

Eleanor saw in a moment that this was her only chance. She spun the wheel wildly, and let the wind grab a hold of the airship. She heard gunshots fire after her, but it was dark and they flew wide. The cloud of dragonflies—now only four in number—came back to her, perching on her shoulders. The wind had its way with the airship, dragging it away and smothering it with clouds.

Eleanor slumped down on the deck and let her head fall into her hands. As she wept the eddies and currents of the air played with the ship. This tumult would give her some advantage. By the time they had prepared and stoked the engines of larger airships, she would be on her way.

They would think that she would set course for the City of Swans and the comfort and refuge of her brothers. They would never guess that the princess was in fact aiming the airship for the City of Eagles—the traditional enemy of her home.

Finally, after shedding her tears, she crawled to her feet, and made her way to the engine room to stoke the boiler to life. She had never piloted an airship, but her memory of traveling on her father's ships served her well.

Still it took two days to find her way to her destination. They were chill, frightening days, in which she sat on deck rummaging through the two bags of tools that Stella had collected, and scanning the diagrams they had done. Her head felt stuffed and overfull. The idea that she was going to have to do this thing alone was enough to drive her brain to distraction.

It was almost a relief when the city itself came into view. The City of Eagles Eleanor had read much of, but naturally never seen for herself. Unlike the carnival of colours of the City of Swans, the Eagle airships wore cloth of silver on every single envelope. In the morning's light the collection that made up the city gleamed like the light's in her father's ballroom.

"No," Eleanor whispered to herself, using up her voice while she still could. "I mustn't think of father. Only my brothers—they deserve my thoughts."

It also helped to think of Madame Escrew, and her face if she could just complete her task. That would be a sweet return.

The ferry was accompanied into the city by a squadron of ornithopters. Eleanor stood at the wheel, her mouth dry, and followed the shouted instructions of the pilot to follow him in. She couldn't help but contemplate that if these were the City of Eagle's idea of a defensive perimeter then they would have no chance against the mechanical swans Madame Escrew had constructed. It was not just her brothers she would be saving; the City of Eagles and all the others would be saved too.

The squadron guided her towards a small dock, and the workers there helped her tie up her ship. She was lucky in that she was not dressed in anything that bore the emblem of her home and neither did the ferry.

The princess threw the two sacks over her shoulder with a grunt and then stepped out into foreign territory. The dock-master came bustling over to her, wearing a brown coat bearing the eagle crest. "Two ducats a day," he snapped, not meeting her eyes, but instead scribbling down notes on the ferry.

"Actually," Eleanor interrupted him, "I am looking to sell it and take up lodgings in the city."

The dock-master's sharp blue eyes darted up to meet hers. "Lot of that these days. You should find Master Pettingren on the lower docks. He's been buying up airships of all sizes. People appear to think war is coming. We've had to lash in three dozen new ships this month at least."

Eleanor shuddered. The Cities grew a little, but that many new arrivals seeking the perceived safety of the Eagle meant that the free travellers of the skies were also getting nervous.

She had to hurry. She sold the stolen ferry to the thin, but remarkably cheery Master Pettingren very easily, and earned a healthy sack of ducats; even in a time of approaching war a ship was still an expensive object. Then she found herself a small workshop in the lower hull of an airship hulk.

It was full of desperate people, packed into tiny rooms in the lumbering ship. The place ran with gossip and contagion in equal amounts. Again, Eleanor forced herself to ignore all that. Instead she set herself to the calculations of what she would need. Then the princess went into the city and bought the strands of silver that Stella had said were required for the cloaks. She bought all she could find, but by her calculations she knew that it would only be enough for six cloaks. She would have to venture out later and find more.

Still it was surprisingly cheap. That she had not expected.

Once she said thank you to the shop owner and gathered up her materials, she knew that had to be the last time she spoke. It was too important a task that she couldn't leave anything to chance. Stella had told her the magic and the crafting would require everything she had. She would have to give it that.

As she returned to her little cell, she weighed the remaining coins in her pocket. She hoped they would be enough to not only buy the remaining silver she would need, but also to purchase the things a human body needed as well. Silver might be cheap in the City of Eagles, but food was not.

She would just have to do the best she could. In her cell she laid out all the tools from the two canvas bags. There were various sizes of little saw, some with diamond blades, a set of gleaming screwdrivers that tingled in her fingertips. And then there were the starlight opals.

Eleanor sat back on her heels. She had been thinking what might be required to interfere with the workings of the swan machines, and though she had many ideas it was the use of the opals that she was really guessing at. Their function was something Stella had not had time to explain. That was the sticking point, and the one thing she was least confident about.

However, doubts had to be left behind. First, Eleanor laid out and measured the silver tape, and hoped her calculations were correct. She had only the glimpses of the swan machines she's managed to catch from the prison window, and so was forced to rely on her own sense of size to go by.

The clockwork underneath of the cloaks was the easiest part for her to do. She designed spikes that would drive into the workings of the mechanical swans, locking the skins on them tight—this was just in case Madame Escrew had set some defences on her devices. The skins that would hold these mechanics were by far the harder to construct. The silver tape was flexible, but reluctant to give itself up to her. She knew that she had to weave the skin in just the right way. It had to be strong and yet conform to a shape.

The solution she settled on was one that drew inspiration from ancient Armor—the kind that she had seen on display in paintings in her father's palace. It was called fish Armor, though no one in any city had seen a fish for ten generations.

First she fixed the silver tape into a tiny loop of no greater circumference than she could make with her index finger and thumb. The next loop she threaded through the first and welded it shut. It was long, tiresome work that made her head, her eyes and her fingers ache. It would have been nice to spare a curse word now and then; but she was careful never to do that. Always in her mind was the witch's reminder that she needed to put everything into it.

She ate little with her stinging fingers, but still ventured out to buy what silver she could find. A princess had no experience at thievery, and dare not risk being caught—that would mean an end to her project. So instead she bought what little cheap food could be found. Though in times of war there was little enough of that.

So as the days and weeks went past, Eleanor's figure began to dwindle, and her mind grew foggy with hunger. Now the cloak making was going on by shear habit.

The role of the starlight opals was something that still eluded her, until she was passing—or rather staggering—through the market and saw an aristocratic lady with a cloak wrapped around her against the chill. Eleanor's head jerked up, and her gaze followed the woman. Her garment was festooned with glimmering beads. Despite her weariness and hunger, she knew this would be the best way to add the opals to her own project.

She wobbled her way back to her dim rooms, and set to work immediately.

However, a strange young woman, who communicated with gestures alone, had made an impression in a city on the verge of all-out war. Gossip was not something that Eleanor had calculated in her plans.

She was working at the inner cage of the fourth cloak, when the flimsy door was kicked in. She hadn't eaten in three days, but somehow she managed to hold back a scream, or any other sound.

"There she is—the witch!" The voice seemed to fill the tiny room, and Eleanor staggered a little as she rose to her feet. Her tools scattered on the floor, and she thought how in the sky she was going to find them again.

Guardsmen struggled to enter such a small space, but all of them were pointing and shouting. None of them used the word 'Swan' for which she was very grateful. Still 'witch' was not that much better. In a world constructed on floating airships bound together, the punishment was to see if the witch could fly. If she plummeted to her death then she was obviously innocent, if she did not then she would be weighed with stones until she did.

Eleanor stood tall and for a second almost spoke. Her mouth dropped open, but then she shut it with a snap. Her brothers' fate and that of all the cities that flew the skies depended on her strength of will. It would be weak of her to falter now.

"It is as they say," one burly guardsman rumbled. "She does not speak... even in her own defence."

The word 'witch' was passed from man to angry man, and Eleanor knew there was no way out of this situation. They were blocking her exit from the room, and where could she go without her works anyway?

The four dragonflies buzzed and snapped on her windowsill, but the princess gestured them back. They would only create a worse situation. Brave little insects that they were, she didn't want them destroyed.

Then a voice from the back snapped, "Make way, make way!"

Suddenly the guardsmen were shifting, jostling, and some of them slipping out of the tiny room. They all hurriedly got out the way to make space for the man who demanded entry.

Eleanor was sure she was hallucinating. Though she did not know the tall young man, with the military uniform who loomed in the doorway, she did recognize the silver badge on the scarlet sash over his shoulder. It was an eagle, with its wings spread. Only one person could wear such a thing. She had seen its like only on her father.

This was the King of the City of Eagles. Eleanor wobbled on her feet, as her stomach growled, and her brain struggled to catch up. This was the last person she wanted to seem weak in front of, but going so long on so little food finally caught up with her.

Eleanor's vision blurred as her legs buckled. She tried desperately to prop herself up against the wall, but it was treacherous and she ended up sliding to the floor. Throughout it all, she kept her jaw locked shut, refusing to let out even a pained sigh.

Through her greying vision, she saw the King bend down towards her. He had startling eyes; they gleamed gold like a hawk's. He turned and commented over his shoulder, "She doesn't much look like a witch to me. And most certainly not a very good one."

"But sire, you know the temple will..." from her place on the floor she couldn't tell who spoke.

Darkness was washing over her, but the last thing that Eleanor heard was the King's word, "We must keep an eye on her, that is for certain."
*****

When Eleanor returned to consciousness, it was to find herself in a bed as soft as the one she had left back in the Swan City. For a moment, a blissful moment, she believed she had imagined the whole horrible Madame Escrew event, but then as she sat up, she realized that she was not in the city of swans, but one of eagles. It was the decorations that told her that immediately.

Great birds of prey were shown everywhere; in tapestries, paintings, and most disturbingly of all in sculpture, where a spread-winged eagle had a tormented swan in its claws.

That bought her back to reality with a start. So she slid out of bed, and gently to her feet. Immediately, the smell of food on a nearby table drew her over. Eleanor had devoured all of the soup and bread, before she even worked out it was onion broth and good millet bread.

Feeling her brain starting to work, like a furnace finally fed coal, she began to explore. The room was decorated in outrageously rich fashion— even more so than she was used to in her home. It was a two room suite of some kind. Eleanor entered cautiously to find the second room was an observatory. Her father had one very similar in his own palace. This was however even larger, filled with many long benches, and on these were all her tools, the cloaks in progress. Even the starlight opals were there and the four little mechanical dragonflies.

She rushed over and ran her hands over them to make sure she was not imagining it.

"I think you will find everything there," the prince, standing in the window, overlooking the swirling clouds, had gone all unnoticed by her.

A hundred questions bubbled in her mind, but she managed to hold them back.

"I imagine you are wondering," the King said, stepping closer, those emerald eyes locked on her, "why I would give you this chance to complete your work, when you might be some kind of witch."

Eleanor looked away, totally unsure how to deal with a man without her tongue.

"Well," he said, picking up the jar of starlight opals, "You are a most unusual one, and I think perhaps you are silent by choice." The look he shot her was direct and probing.

The princess had never felt such a wash of warmness over her body for a man's sake. Certainly there had been suitors in her time, but as the sole sister in a line of eleven brothers, not many had lingered long. Now she wished most fervently for the freedom to use her voice; show him her wit and intelligence. Instead, all she could do was smile. Even writing was something she dare not attempt.

The King shook his head, as if emerging from a deep pool of water. "But where are my manners? I have not properly introduced myself! I am King Nikolai Swoop, of the City of Eagles." His fingers tweaked the cravat almost nervously.

A little confused herself, Eleanor picked up an end of the silver metallic tape, and gestured for his permission to begin. The little ticking of the clock in her head reminded her she had little time for embarrassment—or any other emotion come to think of it.

Nikolai tilted his head. "They say I should see if you fly, but I am preparing a city for war from the King of the Swans, and I cannot turn down this chance to see what you are building. None of my tinkers can fathom what this is all about. Maybe it can help my city survive."

He seated himself on a stool near the window, out of her way, but near enough that he could observe what Eleanor was doing. And thus they proceeded.

He came and watched her every day while the dragonflies circled the observatory. Sometimes he sat silent; departing without a word after no particular length of time. She imagined he had many things to deal with since they were—as he said—on the very edge of war. Part of her—the smallest portion that she allowed freedom in those brief moments she stopped to eat—was flattered at the King's attention.

For there were times he talked. At first they were words of a ruler; light matters of court, moments of his family history, and the minutiae of ruling that grated on him. As the days passed though he delved deeper, and perhaps emboldened by her silence, told her things about himself. He revealed his fears, his hopes and dreams.

For herself, Eleanor yearned to tell him the same, but the work and the magic held her tongue.

The mechanical delivery system was ready—well as ready as it was ever going to be, but it was the cloaks that would wrap tight around the forms of the swan machines that were the most time consuming.

As she sat on the floor, her fingers worn almost to nubs by the work, Eleanor's mind contemplated the thousand ways that this could have been made easier. If she had the voice she could have asked Nikolai to get some of his subjects to help—but Stella had asserted that it must be done by the princess alone. Once when her fingers started bleeding, Nikolai tried to take the link work away from her and do it himself. Her frantic dismay had been enough apparently to keep from trying that again. He did however remind her to eat.

As she marked the twenty-first day off on the wall of her prison—something that made the King's brow furrow with confusion—Eleanor sighed.

Nikolai looked up from where he sat, in the sun, his gold hair gleaming. He looked so normal and wonderful, that Eleanor risked another sigh. She slid down to the floor once more and picked up the cloak.

Despite her protestations, the cloaks were nearly done. In fact she was working on the final one, and confident that she was going to finish it well before the end of the month and the deadline that Stella had set. She only had to stay the course and finish the final loop work, as dull and painful as that was.

All would have been well, had the bells not begun to ring. It was not in a happy way, but in a discordant chorus that spoke of imminent threat. Nikolai leapt to his feet, even as Eleanor ran to the windows.

Together they looked out into a clear blue sky, and the princess felt her chest tighten and her throat close. The machines were so much more incredible and frightening when seen in the daylight.

Great wings of brass and bronze beat the air as the eleven swans descended on the City of Eagles. Eleanor and Nikolai watched as the city's ornithopters flitted out to meet them. Compared to the stout realism of the machines, the 'thopters looked like a child's set of paper planes. They lasted just about as long.

The elegant swan necks were bent towards the attackers. Above the desperate ringing of the bells, could be heard a dreadful, constant stream of explosions. "Holy steam," he swore, thumping the back of the chair.

The delicate wings of the ornithopters caught fire and crisped. Their descent was silent and dreadful.

"Wait here!" The King grabbed her shoulders, and planted a kiss on Eleanor's silent mouth. It was sudden, unexpected and made her blood rush to her head, but before she could react further, he darted out the door to see to his city.

The princess was left standing in the conservatory, the final cloak trailing from her fingers, and watching her brothers destroy a city she had come to see was no enemy. Eagle and Swan had been at odds for generations, but it had never broken out into real war.

Some of the smaller airships were punctured already. Their envelopes sagging and collapsing in on themselves. People on the deck below ran backwards and forwards like disturbed insects, cutting the ties between the stricken ships and those still untouched; trying to save them. It seemed like a pointless attempt to Eleanor because soon enough the whole city would be in flames.

The princess knew, despite one of the cloaks not being completely done, that this was the only chance she would have. She cast about, grasped hold of a chair, and flung it through the nearest window of the observatory. It shattered, spraying glass out into the void, and the sound joined the screaming of the citizens and the rattle of the swan machines.

"There she is!" The guardsmen had entered the workroom, and at their head was a priest of the Sky God in his bright blue vestments. He looked as though he was about to have apoplexy right there and then.

"Witch!" He howled, his pointing managing to encompass both Eleanor and the devastation beyond the window. "She has bought these demons of the air down on us."

Eleanor knew she only had mere moments and that all of her work of the last weeks hung on this few heartbeats. The four dragonflies, quiet for so many weeks, flew once more to her defence. Eleanor flung another chair at the advancing guards and spun away.

Then as they scrambled towards her she turned to the window and screamed. "Brothers! Brothers!"

Something in her blood, something in the bond they shared must have reached them, because the machines turned. For a long second they flapped in position, outlined against the bright blue sky, with the flame light of the airships below them reflected on their brass wings. Then, they dived.

The priest and the guards screamed behind her, leaping back almost as quickly as they had surged forward. Eleanor stood there, one cloak held in each hand and waited.

The swan machines, each about twice the size of a man, crashed through the glass of the observatory. Eleanor could see that her memory had not failed her. The details of the gears and workings of the swans were as she had seen it in the moonlight.

The swans all bent their heads to her, and she could see the weapons that Madame Escrew had fitted them with: devices to spurt flame, and repeating guns the like of which she had never seen. All of which could be turned on her in a moment.

If the remains of her brothers were truly gone then this would be her last moment. Eleanor stood poised, knowing that she didn't have any chance should they turn on her. The articulated necks, and gleaming jewelled eyes of the birds were all directed at the princess below.

"Come away…" Nikolai's voice came soft from behind her back. He sounded like he was calming a falcon, trying to put a hood on it.

Eleanor dare not glance back at him, one sight of his face twisted with concern and she would be quite undone. Yet she couldn't tell him what to do, not yet…not when she was so close to the end of her task. She just had to hope he would follow her lead.

With quick strides, she walked towards the first of the swans, and flung the cloak over the metallic back. With eleven brothers she had to work fast, but then she heard the King himself step up and help her. He couldn't have known what he was doing, but her heart swelled at his trust in her.

Finally, the swans all stood, covered in their cloaks.

"See my liege," said the temple priest, finally collecting himself, "the witch knows them."

"I think perhaps she does," Nikolai held up his hand, to stay the guards from making a move.

Eleanor took out of her pocket the largest starlight opal. The one worth a fortune in any kingdom. Every love meant sacrifice.

Dropping the gem to the floor, she pulled her mallet out from her other sleeve and bought the weight of it smashing down on the precious thing.

The white light within was freed, making everyone in the room flinch away. All except Eleanor, who watched it fill all the other gems in the cloaks. They gleamed brightly, bringing power to her creations. She heard the creak of the gears, and the snap of the vices within as they locked tight on the structure of the swans. The machines threw their proud heads back, and great trumpeting screams broke the rest of the remaining glass in the observatory.

The machines shivered, the workings within shaking themselves loose, something large and metallic ground against itself. And then, the doors burst open and Eleanor's brothers—all eleven of them—staggered from within.

They were gaunt, pale and sweaty, but Eleanor didn't care. She rushed to them, called their names, embraced them.

After so long in silence her voice cracked, and fractured on the words. Then she felt Nikolai's hand on her shoulder, and now she found she could look up into the King's eyes. She was free of subterfuge and the tenets of the cloak construction.

"These are my brothers." It felt so good to say it, though it came out husky. "I am sure you are wondering. Madame Escrew has my father in thrall, and she did this to them. The machines were swallowing them, and I had to work in silence to free them."

"That was not what I was wondering," Nikolai replied. "Your name is what I have wanted all this time?"

She smiled, as she helped Brian to his feet. "Eleanor."

The princess and the King stared at each other, while the brothers shook themselves and blinked.

The priest had turned white, while the guardsmen shifted on their feet uncertain what to do. They could all tell that something had changed in the broken observatory.

"Now what do we do Eleanor? What is the next move?" Alan pushed his hair out of his eyes, and she was aware that all of her brothers were once again looking to her for answers.

The King of the Eagles too was watching her; those green eyes expecting and welcoming. She turned and looked at the remains of the swan machines with an analytical eye.

"I say that we can learn a great deal from these machines, and then," she smiled archly, "We turn her work on her, and take back the Swan City and my father."

The men around her nodded.

"And you shall lead us," Nikolai said, taking her hand. "A true Queen of the Swans."

Aladdin
and
His Wonderfully Infernal Device

TEE MORRIS

ONE

Perhaps the marketplace at noon was not the best place to be—at least when you were poor. Since you had no goods to trade, no money for food, nothing more than your wits and the clothes upon your back, you tended to notice the more unpleasant smells, sounds, and sights of the bazaar. Instead of succulent smoked meats or the brilliance of silks both catching the hot Arabian breeze, you tended to notice the smell of goat shit and the pleas of blind beggars.

For Aladdin, however, while hunger roiled in his belly, his senses were trained upon one shop, one keeper, and one essential item. As if it were the Tear of Allah itself the polished wheel sat before the workbench, amidst the other parts of the desk clock. Obviously the artisan felt this morning a need to attract attention to his skills and his business, as he had elected to work in the sunshine. Aladdin had anticipated this, thus he waited in the coolness of the shadows, watching for the moment that would appear. As the sun rose and set, as stars winked to life in the night, and as people bustled about in between these natural regimens, so would Opportunity—the friend and ally of a thief—present itself.

What was important—as an exceptional thief such as Aladdin would say—was to recognize the *right* opening. Too many times, Opportunity would try to lure him out of hiding to play an unkind trick and threaten his capture. Capture would mean the end of his wicked ways, and—provided he survived—a life reliant on generosity. He saw many beggars in the streets, sentenced to one-handed servitude.

Perhaps his fellow vagrants would scoff, *"Serves them right. They were too slow"*, but Aladdin knew the truth. They had been too *quick*. Too quick to judge. Quick to think that Opportunity was beckoning, when in fact it was merely a deceptive shade. Already Aladdin had seen two such false openings, so in the darkness of his favorited hiding place he remained.

There. A customer, fascinated with the clockmaker's work. A conversation struck.

Aladdin's eyes returned to the palm-sized wheel; its cogs glinting in the light of a Persian sun. The merchant's attention was preoccupied, but the timing—and that made Aladdin smile a bit—remained off. He needed to wait. Just a few more seconds…

Then came applause, followed shortly by a small crush of people. Aladdin slipped deftly between children, mothers, and men, all chattering pleasantly about the magician's talents, and how his reputation had more than been upheld. Most impressive; even from as far as Africa, the Great and Powerful Jaha had found such devoted followers.

Aladdin emerged on the other side of the corporeal flow, and soon his palm was bathed in the sun-baked warmth of a polished brass gear.

He saw no shadow or swath of linen stir, he felt no vice grip around his arm; there was nothing but the throng of people, and the movement reminding him of the Karun after a heavy rain.

However, the rushing river never made a sound like this: *"Stop! Thief!"*

Time to run, whispered Opportunity's deceptive twin.

The gear's teeth bit into his hand as his fingers tightened around it. His shoulder pressed against the mass of flesh around him. Women called out, and children cried as they were shoved aside. He couldn't look back—at least not straight away. First, he needed distance, and then he could formulate a way out of the city.

Aladdin felt a couple push into him from behind, alerting him that there was someone on his heels. He now ducked lower and weaved like a thread through the eyes of many needles. He could hear some people in his wake losing their balance, which was good—obstacles for his pursuers—until the crowd suddenly thinned and his steps grew wider. He pumped his legs and darted into an alleyway. The more he ran, the stronger the smell of fish grew. He could hear the calls of dockhands. He was close.

The walls on either side of him disappeared, and he now ran alongside the collection of junks and dhows expelling their riches. Aladdin ducked underneath palettes slowly rising into the air, his eyes still looking for the right cargo. Behind him, the rhythmic pounding of footsteps grew louder and closer.

Aladdin glanced to the right and then followed his gaze. His sudden turn was matched, but he had anticipated they would keep pace with him.

It would be his next move that would test their mettle.

His legs continued to pedal even after he had leaped off the dock. The world opened up around him, then suddenly cool air off the water caressed his skin. His stomach lurched as he tried to catch his breath. Aladdin was falling. Such a curious sensation.

His fingers caught netting and his other hand, still clinging onto the gear wheel, swung up. The treasure's teeth dug into the thick hemp of the cargo net as his legs found purchase. Over the sound of his own deep breaths, he heard the whine of motors compensating for the sudden change in weight, but still Aladdin climbed. He leaned to one side and felt the cargo list. Luckily, it turned him away from the four men now lowering rifles as he ascended over them and into the rooftops.

Aladdin looked around him and watched as the cargo now swung over a building. The men below began calling for the guards still on the ground. With his breathing now under control and his muscles burning, he started to scale down the bulbous collection of crates. The dockhands were gathering under Aladdin, perhaps hoping to earn an extra coin or two from his capture. His arms trembled, but still he waited.

When two men reached for him, the young boy pushed, tucking his legs up to his chest. He rolled back and when his legs shot out, he sent one dockhand sprawling into his comrades. The hand clutching the gear swung before him, slicing into the cheek of the other closing on him. When he too fell away, Aladdin sprang forward, through the opening in the men and across the space to another rooftop. He continued across the rooftop and jumped again. It was when he reached the sole door on this rooftop that he stopped and looked back.

The guards were now on the edge of the first building, their eyes madly darting back and forth.

With a grin, Aladdin wrenched the door open and thundered down the stairs. Perhaps a head turned to follow his descent, but at this point he didn't care; let them look. He was merely a shadow now, and soon he would be nothing but a wisp of sand disappearing in the wind.

He stopped at the door, took a breath, and tucked the still-warm gear wheel inside his sash.

Now it was time to find something to eat. He turned.

The man standing in the doorway did not wear the stern look or the standard uniform of the Sultan, but he looked large enough to be a part of the army. The boy could see a thick, sturdy frame under his robes, especially as his arms were crossed over his chest. His dark eyes considered Aladdin; the longer he looked at him the broader his smile became.

"After an impressive escape like that," he said, his voice rumbling like a distant thunderstorm from off the sea, "you must be hungry."

"Famished," Aladdin answered.

The stranger nodded. "You have his spirit—that is most evident." He stepped back and motioned down the street, in the opposite direction from the docks. "Come. Let us find some lunch."

As they walked through the street, Aladdin noticed that the many people of the marketplace were pausing. In fact, many of them were staring. In a few instances gatherings actually *parted* to make way for the two of them. Aladdin looked over his shoulder for soldiers or even an honour guard, but all he saw were people in their wake, pointing at them, and wearing the most brilliant of smiles.

Sweet, savoury scents of cardamom, curry, and garlic now filled his nostrils. On cue, his stomach rumbled impatiently. Aladdin was indeed famished. He considered making an escape only after this stranger paid for a meal.

"Ah, Great Jaha," a gentleman gabbled as they walked into his dining establishment, "you honour me with your patronage!"

Aladdin blinked. "Jaha? The magician?"

His companion didn't respond to Aladdin but kept his attention on the shopkeeper. "Yes, Karim, such a pleasure to step into your fine establishment." Jaha motioned to Aladdin, as if presenting him formerly. "My associate and I are more than ready for a meal. Please, only your best."

Karim recognized Aladdin straightaway—as Aladdin recognized him—but the café owner's outward disdain disappeared as quickly as water under the noonday sun. His eyes went from Aladdin to the magician.

"This is your associate?" His brow creased in confusion.

Jaha lifted an eyebrow. "There is no problem with the company I choose to keep, is there?"

The restaurant owner shuddered. "Magister, forgive my impertinence, please," he replied with a flourish, bestowing formal obeisance.

Aladdin followed Jaha to a small booth that isolated them from the rest of the patrons. Several took a pause in eating to watch them. Once they had taken their seats, the wooden pillar set within the wall of the establishment opened up. Mechanical arms presented a tea that was tepid enough to be soothing but not uncomfortable when combined with the day's heat. They had only taken a few sips when a chime rang softly. From above their heads, a tray lowered and the mechanical arms now offered "manna from Heaven"—as the infidel crusaders from Europe would say—in the form of jasmine rice, soft flatbread, lamb and goat, seasoned by spices Aladdin only knew from scraps he scavenged.

"And they call me a magician," Jaha chortled as the metal arms retracted from their table and returned to the kitchen above their heads. They both watched as the staff there replaced the hole in the ceiling with a new plate. "I suppose the Europeans are good for some things after all." He then motioned to the food before them. "I don't stand on ceremony, boy. Eat!"

It did not take long for Aladdin to stuff his mouth with bread and lamb. He only paused when he realized that Jaha was looking at him disapprovingly.

"I said 'eat' not 'devour.' Finish what food you have in your mouth," he said, tearing off a piece of bread and dipping it into a small bowl of yogurt, "and then watch and learn, boy."

Aladdin doubted the magician had ever known what it was like to be hungry. That did not mean Jaha had been wrong in correcting him; Aladdin had been fairly gluttonous. As he chewed and chewed at the huge amount of food stuffed in his mouth, his cheeks burned with embarrassment as Jaha continued to slowly, meticulously savour the food before them. The magician seemed highly amused by Aladdin's struggle.

When he finally managed to choke down his mouthful, Aladdin asked, "Why are you helping me?"

Jaha's smile—the one he had worn when he had met him in the street—returned. "Why wouldn't I wish to treat my own family to a much-needed, well-earned meal?"

Aladdin felt a sharp twinge in his chest. "Family?"

The magician stopped his hand half-raised to his mouth. "What is your name, boy?"

"Aladdin."

"A good name, most fitting for our family," he said with a hint of warmth in his voice. "Well, Aladdin, I will not mince words with you—I am your father's brother, finally come home."

An invisible hand felt as if it had clasped around his neck. His mother had never mentioned an uncle, let alone any sort of remote connection with the famous magician, the All-Powerful Jaha. They had a simple life—as simple as any of those who served at the Sultan's pleasure. Aladdin knew he complicated that life with his antics; his mother always scolded him for his reckless ways. She cursed his lost father's name, especially at moments when Aladdin would arrive home short of breath and wearing the sweat of a day's mischief on his skin.

Never had his mother told him of an uncle. Never had she hinted that uncle was the All-Powerful Jaha.

"I was sold into bondage when your father was only three," Jaha began, "so it comes as no surprise that he did not remember or speak of me. He knew me by a different name, of course."

Aladdin tipped his head to one side. "Your name isn't really Jaha?"

"A story we should save for another time, but in brief," he said popping a few small berries into his mouth, "I was taught to pick locks by another slave. He had been quite clever this gent; he taught me sleight-of-hand and other illusions to pass the hours."

"He could pick locks? Then why did he not escape?"

Jaha took a sip of tea, and continued. "He had for some reason he never explained, made me a ward of sorts. This meant we would escape together and split a small fortune that he had amassed before his own misfortune."

"A likely story," Aladdin snorted before helping himself to a piece of goat. He wrapped a piece of the soft bread around it. "So what happened to your teacher?"

"He died in the midst of our escape."

Aladdin looked up from his morsel in mid-bite. Jaha was staring out of a window at the far end of the restaurant.

"Nassir gave me the location of his fortune with his dying breath, and I went in search of it, our master and his dogs on my heels. I knew if I wanted to truly be free, I needed a new life and that day Jaha was born." He chuckled as he picked up his own tea. "The All-Powerful bit did not come to be until I began to travel. I had the skills of a talented thief, but instead I found a more 'honest' life in the pursuits of an illusionist."

"A magician, you mean," Aladdin pressed.

"Come, come, Aladdin," Jaha chided. "You hardly believe in such nonsense as magic, séances, and the like, do you?" He shook his head. "In my travels I have met many interesting people, but it was a Frenchman named Robert-Houdin that opened my eyes at what many perceived as 'magic.' He helped refine and sharpen my skills; not only in my illusions but also in my relationships with my fellow man. You saw how I knew the master of this house?"

Aladdin nodded.

"In fact I only knew of his name—but knowing a man's name can grant you entrance into his home. It is these talents of society that aided me in my advancement. Something I would very much like to pass unto you— when you are ready," he said to Aladdin with a wink before continuing his story. "Once I had made a name for myself, I set out to fulfil a promise; to reunite with my brother."

Aladdin hung his head.

Jaha nodded. "As I feared." He looked Aladdin over, "You are what— fourteen?"

"Sixteen," Aladdin insisted.

"Of course, your smaller size—I should have known." He nodded, finished his tea, and rose from the table. "What of your mother?"

"She still makes carpets for the palace," he replied, tearing another slice of flatbread in half as he stood.

"Take me to her," he said. "It is time I make amends to my lost family."

Aladdin watched in awe as the magician thanked the owner without paying a single coin for the fine meal.

Jaha tilted his head. "His payment is in my presence there. People saw us go in, people saw us leave, our bellies full, our faces smiling contentedly. His business will prosper." His smile glowed against his darkened skin. "That is not magic, but something far more powerful—the testimony of the All-Powerful Jaha." He winked at him and then nodded. "Now, I wish to see my sister."

TWO

Mother!" Aladdin cried. "Mother!"

Her hands lowered from the lamp above her head as he entered the humble dwelling. The second lamp already burning signalled she was anticipating a long night and a large amount of work.

"Well, well, my clever son, what steals your breath so at the end of the day?" Her tone grew mirthless as she added, "I heard a story about some commotion by the docks. A young thief swift of foot enjoyed a quick escape from the Sultan's guards."

Aladdin felt his throat tighten, but hearing footsteps behind him, he quickly rediscovered his voice. "Mother, I have a surprise. A blessing! My uncle has found me!"

"Uncle?" His mother barked out a laugh. "Boy, what mischief are you—"

Her words halted at the sight of Jaha. He touched his fingertips to his forehead, his lips, and then his heart.

Jaha's arms opened as he said, "Dearest sister, I present myself to you as your humble servant."

Aladdin's mother stumbled back. "You—you—" she stammered, "—you are the All-Powerful Jaha!"

"And your departed love's brother. Lost for many a year, but sadly come too late after his death."

Aladdin hugged his mother as she fought to catch her breath. "He's not really a magician, but an illusionist," he assured her.

The woman's eyes darted between him and Jaha. "Mustapha never mentioned a brother..."

"As I told your industrious son here, I was taken from our family when he was very young. Perhaps he remembered me as a shade, a distant memory, but I never forgot him." He motioned to a seat and smiled warmly. "May I?"

Both Aladdin and his mother scrambled to clear a place for him at their small table. With a whisper to his mother, the boy turned to a small hearth and began to boil water for tea.

Behind him, Jaha continued. "My own life, while of late has been quite blessed with fortune, was formerly a tale of misery and woe. Aladdin has heard much of it already. As I was lost to my brother, please forgive me as I ask your name."

Aladdin watched his mother blush; truly a rare sight to behold. "Farrin."

"Farrin," he repeated, his eyes seemed to catch the light of the nearby lamp. "I can only beg you to forgive me for my failure in not contacting you sooner. I hope you do not mind that I called upon young Aladdin here first."

Her hand went to her mouth. Aladdin paused when a muffled sob escaped his mother. When she spoke, he felt his skin prickle. "Oh dear brother, it is I who must beg of forgiveness for the shame that haunts our family is all on account of my boy."

Her son spun around. "Mother, no! You make so very little as a rug maker for the Sultan and for the merchants of Bagdad! What I do I must so that we can survive!"

"You shame your father's name with your mischief!" Farrin spat over her shoulder.

"Farrin, Aladdin, please…"

They were silenced by the gentle plea. Jaha looked upon them both, his expression not piteous but more regretful.

"I blame myself for your strife," he said, his soft, soothing voice filling the confines of their home. "I should have come sooner, taken a more authoritative role in my brother's affairs, but I had not the opportunity to call upon you."

Aladdin stared at the All-Powerful Jaha. His mind repeated over and over again—that this was the great Jaha prostrate before them. He looked over to his mother, and she was as equally dumbstruck.

"Please, Farrin, let me begin to make amends; let me take Aladdin as an apprentice. The boy is of an age where he should come to discover his path, his destiny." Aladdin's mother gasped and clapped her hands to her mouth as Jaha continued, "Our journey, if it so please you, would start tonight—after you have eaten."

Aladdin scuttled in front of his mother and dropped to his knees. "Please, Mother, please! Let me do this!"

On many occasions Aladdin had seen his mother cry, usually on account of his thievery—but this was the first time her tears were ones of joy. He placed his hand on her cheek, and she leaned into it.

"Oh, Aladdin, you are so like your father. I tried so hard to guide you, but I always knew your gifts were not meant for an ordinary life."

"I could see that in his little rooftop adventure this afternoon," Jaha said, his smile approving and perhaps a bit mischievous.

His mother arched a brow. "So…"

"Mother, please, are you going to spoil this moment of happiness?"

"Thinking about it," she quipped.

A laugh suddenly bubbled out from her. This was his punishment then—a tweak of his nose.

"It's settled then?" Jaha asked, rising from his place. "A lovely farewell dinner for your mother, and then we are off, the two of us, yes?" He clapped his hands together. "Gather what you will need, Aladdin, as we will leave from the restaurant."

"Yes, Master," Aladdin said, just before disappearing deeper into the small house. When he returned he carried a small haversack over one shoulder and another pack which covered his entire back.

"What in the name—" Jaha began.

"Oh, Aladdin, certainly you cannot mean to lug that infernal device on your travels."

"Mother, it is nearly done!" he protested. "I can finish it whilst we travel."

"You have me most curious, Aladdin," Jaha said, then motioned to the outside where night was falling quickly.

"Fine, bring it with you, but—" Aladdin's mother said, her slender finger pointing at her son, "it stays outside the restaurant."

"I can't do that," Aladdin began, pulling the covered pack closer to him. "There are thieves in the city."

He couldn't understand why Jaha and his mother found his concerns so funny. They were both, in fact, moved to tears.

The three of them were quite the sight as they walked through the streets. A local rug maker, a street whelp carrying an odd contraption across his back, and a world-renown magician.

As they went, Jaha wanted to hear more about his departed brother, and his mother remained curious about the life Aladdin would be living under his care. The words they traded were just that to him—words. Aladdin surrendered himself to ideas he had once reserved for dreams. Everything was changing before him. His uncle was *an illusionist!* Aladdin knew of these men and their need for ingenious machinations. His dreams were now about to take form. Full form. Something tangible. Something wonderful.

He was still quite full from lunch; so while his mother and uncle talked, laughed, and celebrated, Aladdin stared at the covered device by his feet. He then felt a slight pressure on his stomach and gave a little chuckle. The prize from earlier that day was still there, waiting. He breathed a sigh of relief. Since meeting Jaha, everything had been a blur.

"Aladdin."

He blinked, nearly jumping at the sound of his name. The conversation had paused between Jaha, his mother, and what appeared to be a small group of followers of Jaha. All eyes were upon him, and Aladdin felt his skin grow hot.

"Forgive me, uncle," he spoke. The strange sensation of being the centre of attention he found he didn't particularly like.

"No need, my apprentice," Jaha said proudly. "Were you having a vision of the future?"

His uncle did understand him. "Yes, Master. I think I was."

Jaha chuckled, encouraging those gathered to laugh with him. "Excellent, my clever apprentice. This is why I have come home, and we must not waste away our time together. I do have one more performance before your great Sultan in the Imperial Theatre tomorrow, but tonight I have business elsewhere that cannot wait. We must be off." The crowd groaned in protest, but Jaha held his hands up, shaking his head slowly. "I did promise myself that I would not keep Aladdin from the opportunities that away him and twilight is upon us. Come, my apprentice, for you have much to learn."

As Jaha gave blessings to his followers, Aladdin stepped aside with his mother.

"I will not disappoint you," he pledged.

"No, you will not," she assured him. "I know there is much of your father in you, and all you have needed is a purpose. I believe Jaha will give you that purpose."

"Yes," he said, turning to look at his uncle, "I believe my uncle will lead me to great fortune."

"Promise me something, Aladdin," his mother said, the tone in her voice demanding his full attention, "do not dismiss what you have already learned."

Aladdin's brow furrowed. "What do you mean, mother?"

Her dark gaze flicked over to Jaha and then returned back to him. "I mean that even in light of my disapproval, you are far more clever than you realize. You know when danger is close." Her eyes went back to his uncle again, and she added, "As does your mother."

Aladdin did not turn. The strange chill that he felt on meeting Jaha had returned, so intensely that he had to fight down a shudder.

"Go with Jaha. I do not doubt that you will find your destiny as he promises but perhaps not in the fashion that you may imagine."

She wrapped her arms around him, and he could feel it in her embrace. This was goodbye.

This was also an opportunity. "What is it, mother?" he whispered in her ear.

"Your father was one of three children. He had two sisters," she returned, her grip tightened. "There was no brother." They parted as Jaha drew closer. "Be safe, my sweet son."

Aladdin knew the tears in her eyes were sincere. She wanted him to discover why this man wanted him, and she believed in his ability to return home. He was, as she said, a survivor.

"I will, mother. I will."

They both waved in return to the small gathering and their affection. Their collected wishes of luck, prosperity, and opulence continued to echo around them until finally Aladdin and Jaha we surrounded by moonlight and the open deserts.

He held an unlit torch, and turned it base sharply to the left. The bulbous tip erupted into flame.

"We have a few hours of gas within this, so we must make haste," he said to Aladdin. "Come."

Aladdin looked over his shoulder one last time, shifted the contraption across his back once more, and followed Jaha into the darkness.

THREE

"The idea of performing magic in front of so many is a little frightening," Aladdin admitted to the man at his side as they crested a dune.

He had never travelled so far at night across the desert, and he found the quiet most unsettling. Even tucked away in a corner of the city there was always a din. There were people close. Always. Here, in the expanse devouring him, his voice seemed to disappear.

"I'm more used to remaining unseen," he continued. Why wasn't Jaha talking to him? He had become ever so quiet since leaving Baghdad. "I wouldn't call it stage fright so much as a new way of thinking, yes, uncle? Now instead of sleight-of-hand that no one should see, I now must think of how to do what I have always done, but make sure everyone sees me."

Jaha paused, looked to his left, then to his right.

"Yes," Aladdin said, shifting the pack on his shoulders again as he looked over the open void before them, "it will take some getting used—"

The gaslight torch was still high above Jaha's head when he rounded on Aladdin. His face was still mostly concealed in shadow, but the whites of his eyes managed to cut through the void.

"Utter one more word, boy, and I will remove your tongue. Understand?"

Aladdin nodded. He had heard threats before; he knew this was not empty intimidation. What had been spoken was a promise.

He held his gaze with Aladdin for a moment, sniffed, and then returned his gaze back to the horizon. They were atop one of the highest dunes of the desert, and with the moon still full and brilliant in the sky, sand stretched in every direction.

"It must be here," Jaha muttered.

They descended into a valley of sand dunes, the ever-changing mountains on either side of them threatening to block out the moon. Jaha reached into his satchel and produced three polished spheres. He held them in a gloved palm and brought the torch closer to them. The spheres suddenly flashed, and that was when Jaha tossed them up into the air.

Aladdin watched the orbs rocket upward, accompanied by a shrill, high-pitched whistle. When the piercing sound faded off, the patch of night above their heads erupted into green flame. The darkness pulled back like a curtain, and now there were details in the dunes and valley that he could clearly see.

"Quickly, boy," Jaha commanded, pointing in the direction opposite of his own. "You are looking for a large, brass ring—perhaps the size of your chest. We only have moments." His next words resembled the growl of a wild beast. "Do not fail me!"

Aladdin hurriedly looked about, as the emerald luminance around him was already beginning to dwindle. He dug his fingertips in the sand just deep enough to allow him to move through it easily. The valley was long and wider than this light would allow for a proper search. He did not want to state the obvious fact that was now tearing away at his resolve; they were in a desert, in a valley created by sand dunes. Was Jaha expecting these same dunes to be here after the next sandstorm? Who is to say if this fleeting vista was here a month ago, or two?

Then his hand brushed something. It was not a dead animal, nor was it rock. His hand had connected to something large and metallic.

He looked up, and just visible in the shadows and dimming green light was his uncle.

"Your father was one of three children. He had two sisters," his mother had told him in their final embrace. *"There was never any mention of a brother."*

"Uncle!" he called out as his hands began to dig.

The more the curve of the brass ring came into view, the more his mother's words echoed in his ears. Yes, it was true that he had hardly been the most honourable of subjects to the Sultan, but his mother never discouraged his resourcefulness in the streets. She, too, nurtured an instinct based on survival, and perhaps she knew what Aladdin could accomplish with the right opportunity.

He saw it in her eyes when they said goodbye to one another. *You will find your destiny as he promises but not in the fashion that you may imagine.*

"Dig faster, boy!" Jaha snapped at him.

Aladdin did not bother to look up at his false uncle. The façade was beginning to slip. His mother must have suspected there was a method to Jaha, and that Aladdin possessed the means to outwit whatever nefarious intention the man had in store for him.

If only Aladdin were as confident.

His fingers found the base of the ring, and now Aladdin pushed aside the sand until he found an edge. His only light was the moon, but even that was about to disappear. Their torch also seemed to be dwindling.

Another edge. Aladdin dug faster.

Finally, standing in what seemed to be an ankle-deep hole, Aladdin looked across the centre of a hatch matching the width and breath of a small cart. He could move the brass ring back and forth, but with great effort. For this hatch to move, they would need a contraption akin to the locoloaders that had provided him a quick escape on the docks earlier that morning.

"So there you are," Jaha muttered. "Move aside, boy," he said, removing his satchel. "This is where my talents are needed."

Jaha drove the torch into the sand, dug into his bag, and removed four fist-sized spheres. Aladdin squinted in the dim light to watch what Jaha did next. The magician looked at every corner of the massive hatch and then turned a small dial in each of the spheres. He knelt at the corner just by his feet and—*CLANG!* The sphere was impaled on the sharp point of the hatch. Aladdin jumped as—*CLANG!*—Jaha placed a second at the far corner. The man sprinted to the third corner of the hatch—*CLANG!*

As Jaha ran for the fourth and final corner, Aladdin heard a soft, constant *tick-tick-tick-tick* coming from the spheres...

If Jaha had told him to run, Aladdin missed it as he only heard his feet thumping hard against the dunes. He kept Jaha in front of him, the flutter of robes and feel of sand occasionally grazing his skin.

Suddenly the darkness disappeared, and Aladdin was picked up and tossed into Jaha. He felt them both strike sand but never heard their impact on account of the roar coming from behind them.

"Get *off* me, whelp!" Jaha growled, shoving his elbow into the boy's side.

Aladdin rolled back into the sand, but it was not his hard impact against the dunes that stole his breath; it was the incredible sight that bathed the desert in an amazing golden light.

The hatch now cut a dark square in the dunes, but it was disappearing from sight as sand knocked loose was now gradually covering it. Slips of the desert appeared as shimmering veils against a bright yellow light coming from the maw in the valley floor. Aladdin pulled himself up to his feet and joined Jaha at the lip of the opening. The longer they stood there, the brighter the light became. Perhaps it was the removal of the hatch, or the intake of air this chamber now suddenly received, but firelight continued to illuminate the treasure trove before them. Gold. Gems. This was not a king's ransom. This was the ransom of an empire. A dynasty.

Aladdin's reverie was shaken away as Jaha grabbed him by the nape of his neck and spun him around. In the glow of the eternal riches stretching into an unseen horizon beneath them, the magician appeared like a malevolent spirit threatening to hold Aladdin accountable for his crimes in the streets.

"You have done exceedingly well," Jaha spoke, his voice now seeming as sweet as honey from the kitchens of the Sultan himself, "but now we have arrived to your first true test under my care."

Aladdin looked back at the pit and then back to the great shadow looking over him.

"I cannot descend into the cave we have discovered. Agility and age has caught up with me, and such a pursuit as what awaits us in this treasure trove is too much for me." Aladdin flinched as Jaha's hand came to rest on his shoulder. "You must go down into the pit we have unearthed together and follow the cobblestone path within." His grip tightened. "Listen to me carefully, boy—once inside, you will see vessels everywhere overflowing with gold, silver, and the most flawless jewels you would ever see. Do not meddle with them, for if you do death will fall upon you instantly."

"So if I cannot help myself to the treasure here, why am I following this path?" Aladdin spoke. It was a relief to know he had not lost his voice completely.

"You are looking for a lamp."

Aladdin blinked. "A lamp?"

"Yes, a simple brass lamp."

He looked behind his uncle again, taking note of what was just visible—rubies, gold, sapphires, emeralds…

He couldn't help but question, "You're serious?"

Jaha gave a nod and then brought Aladdin to the lip of the pit. "This brass lamp may be alight when you find it. Take the lamp down, put it out, keep it close, and bring it to me." He then gave Aladdin's shoulders a gentle squeeze. "Be brave, be bold, and we shall both be rich all our lives."

The glow of what Aladdin could see now as treasure stretching in all directions bathed them both in amber light. Just within sight at the bottom of the pit was a clearing—a round pattern of cobblestones, completely clean of treasure.

Aladdin turned back to where they had landed and grabbed his strange pack. "I am ready, uncle."

FOUR

The groans and grunts from thirty feet above him were sweet music to Aladdin's ears. If he had not been wearing his pack, there is a good possibility that he would be far lighter and easier to lower into this keep; but this uncle was a false uncle, so he did not mind giving him pain. When Aladdin finally came to the centre clearing, he looked around the massive vault.

Aladdin frowned and muttered, "Who does all this treasure belong to?"

"*Boy!*"

He looked up to see Jaha motioning impatiently from the pit's lip. "Off with you. Remember—do not touch any of the riches around you unless you wish a speedy death!"

"Yes, uncle," Aladdin said, shifting the pack on his back before walking down the path cutting through the vast stores of riches.

Just as Aladdin had observed from above, there were unimaginable treasures on either side of him. He paused at a fountain that was miraculously running with water. The liquid within its basin seemed to sparkle of its own accord. He could tell, just on by looking at it that it was the purest water he would have ever tasted.

Onward, he reminded himself.

After a few more steps, he looked back; the opening where Jaha had lowered him through was now distant and out-of-sight. Aladdin had unknowingly entered some sort of atrium. Its transparent dome was covered with gold coins that reflected a circle of torches within.

Aladdin looked to the opposite end of this chamber and that was when he saw it: the brass lamp, displayed proudly on a simple pedestal. He quickened his pace; and the closer he came to the lamp, the more unimpressive Jaha's desire became.

The item that did make him pause though was something completely different; a thing of beauty.

Much like the lamp Jaha wanted, the device Aladdin stared at was made of brass, but there was also an impressive wood inlay and ornate engravings in the firing mechanism and butt. He reached for the device—but paused. His fingers itched to hold it, but the words of his uncle whispered in his ear. *Do not touch any of the riches around you, unless you wish a speedy death!*

Such was the warning of his uncle. His *false* uncle.

His eyes took in the grappling hook device; truly, a work of art. Aladdin chewed his bottom lip—and then reached out to take up the device's case. He held his breath and waited. His heart continued to beat. The air still smelt of incense. There were no pinches or searing sensations of agony. A deep breath. Then another.

Death had not come for him; at least, not now.

Aladdin removed the grappling hook and coil from its fine velvet case and felt the weight. It was…light; no more than a feather in his palm. The coil did not lend itself too much length, so perhaps the device was not used for scaling buildings. Perhaps a quick escape from window to window, or awning to awning.

He looked back to where Jaha waited for him. If this lamp was the intended bounty for him, perhaps Aladdin could keep this device for his own. Taking it apart to see how it worked would be a treasure in itself.

He fastened the grappling gun to his own sash. It would have been a real delight to have this on hand earlier in the morning.

With a last look at the other riches around him, all of which now felt suddenly obtainable, Aladdin continued to the end of the cobblestones. He stared at the lamp; the flame flickering happily from its tarnished neck.

Aladdin's fingers itched again. *An opportunity*, he thought to himself.

He pointed his grappling device at the lamp. The first click of the trigger extended the teeth of the hook. The next position fired the coil and the teeth clamped on to the lamp's handle. Aladdin threw the gun's switch, and he heard the bow's reel spin. The lamp flew off its pedestal, and its flame disappeared as it sailed through the air into Aladdin's hand.

He held up the lamp, and then considered the grappling gun in his other hand. "No, I won't take you apart right away," he assured the device.

A soft tinkle of metal against metal took Aladdin's attention from the gun to the piles of treasure around him. A gold piece tumbled down a column of coins, triggering other coins to fall. Through his sandals, Aladdin felt bricks shudder. His eyes widened as sand slowly sifted through the hairline cracks between the stones underfoot.

He knew the fear that was threatening to overtake him, but he also knew after many street chases and close calls with the Sultan's guard how to control this fear. Aladdin bent to one knee, casting another glance at Jaha's prize, before removing the shouldered pack he had been carrying all this while.

He cast aside the makeshift cover and flipped the latch that revealed his creation's clockwork. His eyes darted over the many gears, cogs, struts, and springs, a bizarre concert of junk that no one else wanted, and of mechanisms that he obtained through less-than-honest measures and means. His hand slipped to the sash around his waist, and the gear from this morning's adventure was still there, waiting for employment. His fingers made quick work of an empty bolt. As the soft rumble grew, the gear from his morning's exploits was secured in its spindle, the latch locked, and his creation—a device born from stories told by his mother when he was younger—now cantered securely on his back.

He did not anticipate the device throwing his balance off as it did, and the shifting sand now rising as a tide underfoot and the mountains of treasure collapsing around him did even less to keep his pace constant. Aladdin fell to the ground several times in his mad dash back to the opening. He could hear Jaha calling his name.

"Aladdin, you are safe?" The smile the magician gave Aladdin knew was not for him. The young thief could see where his gaze was focused.

"I am!" He grabbed the rope. "And so is your treasure. Pull me up!"

Jaha gave a few tugs at the rope, but Aladdin suddenly felt it go slack. He plummeted back to the cavern, the sand underneath him now decorated with gold and silver baubles.

"I have no footing up here." He laid flat, stretching out his hands. "Throw me the lamp!"

"Stay there, uncle," Aladdin said. "I'll come to you!"

Aladdin ran back in the direction of the path, stopped, and then wrenched hard the cord that dangled from the side of his device. Now joining the clamour of treasure and the rumble of an angry desert was a high pitched whine and rapid ticking. With a hard *snap*, wings of carpet extended to their full length, the beautiful and intricate patterns of his mother's work standing out in dark contrast to the brilliant golden light around him. Aladdin took only three steps until the propeller reached its full rotation and gave the additional lift needed for his wings to send him upward. His uncle flinched but Aladdin managed to grab the man's wrists. He felt himself rise up out of the cave's mouth, but the *pop* from his contraption caused them both to plummet.

Jaha grunted, spraying sand everywhere as Aladdin dangled from the magician's arms, his feet kicking in the open space.

"Give me the lamp, Aladdin," Jaha snarled.

"Pull me up first!" he implored.

"Very well, boy," Jaha said, shifting his weight and then giving a great heave.

Aladdin felt himself inch higher as the wings on his back twitched. Something had stuck in the works. It would require his attention once he was free.

His gaze shot back up to Jaha who was still pulling him free, but only using one hand to do so. Jaha's other wrenched free of Aladdin's hold and reached for where the modest lamp hung. Aladdin tried to roll his body and keep it from him, but his false uncle had grasped it quickly.

The lamp dully caught the light of the cave as Jaha held it over his head. The magician let out a triumphant howl, and Aladdin caught in his eyes a wild, maniacal look that had been there since the cave had been opened.

As Aladdin suspected, once Jaha held the lamp, he wrenched his arm away.

This was why the boy had not removed his grappling hook from the lamp.

Aladdin fell. As he slipped free of the cave's lip, he grabbed the cable still connected to the lamp's handle and tugged. The brass work flew out of Jaha's grasp and returned Aladdin's. He could hear Jaha's scream, the rage of the cave, the collapse of various piles of treasure, and the repetitive *click-click-click* of the contraption on his back. He twisted as he fell, turning in the direction of his desperate yank against his ornithopter's starter cord, and he held his breath as the *click-click-click* turned into a *clack-clack-clack*. He felt himself lurch, and suddenly he swooped up into the air, his body spinning like a top. He was descending deeper into the cave, deeper into the collapsing towers of precious metals, gems and trinkets.

Aladdin twisted the throttle, feeling a surge of heat as the boiler released precious pressure. It helped him get out from under the rich man's avalanche, but it would not help him escape the underground prison.

Aladdin plummeted to the ground, hitting a pile of treasure that scattered bowls and coins everywhere. He pushed up with his arms and looked behind him. Sand from outside was now pouring into the mouth of the cave. The slab that had one been blown clear by Jaha's bombs now slid down the dunes to return to its original resting place. The madness unfolding around him compelled Aladdin to run deeper into the vault, looking for any safe shelter from what appeared to be his fate underneath the sands of the great desert.

FIVE

You will find your destiny as he promises, but perhaps not in the fashion that you may imagine.

His mother's words offered little comfort within the silence of the underground vault with its great hatch now back into place. At least the torches had not extinguished themselves once the cave was sealed. Instead, the lights continued to flicker happily, casting light on what could be all the wealth of the world.

Aladdin emerged from his shelter, a small golden shrine that had probably been hollowed out for a statue or perhaps a sacred urn. He was trapped in a kingdom of wealth, and yet not a scrap of food was in sight.

There was very little of the footpath visible; it was either covered in gold and silver trinkets, or reclaimed by the sand. He had just been grateful the shrine provided a safe haven from the chaos triggered by removing the lamp from its pedestal. Something Jaha failed to mention to him. He promised himself to ask his "mentor" about this oversight when he could.

He was trying to figure out where he was within the cave, but nothing looked as he had originally saw it.

"I am in trouble," he muttered, his own voice the only sound within the massive cavern.

He took a step and felt something bounce against his thigh. He looked down to see the cause of his current strife—the plain brass lamp the All-Powerful Jaha.

Jaha had been more than willing to sacrifice Aladdin to the cave in exchange for the piece of junk. He held it up into the light, considering what was worth the life of another. Perhaps there was an inscription leading to another treasure on it?

Aladdin looked around himself. Greater than this trove?

Then the light caught a pattern; it was no larger than his thumb, but it was a crest or standard of some kind. He had missed that when he first looked at it. The details of the shield were obscured by what appeared to be dried oil or soot.

Aladdin gathered up the end of his sash, spat, and tried to buff away the grime covering the new discovery. He could feel through the fabric the thin engravings, and with each pass of his thumb across the mark, more details were coming into focus.

The signet suddenly popped loose, or it depressed into the lamp. Aladdin could not be certain as when it happened, as a quick, hard jolt of pain shot through his hands, causing him to toss the lamp away. His fingers were tingling, and he felt a little confused and off-balance. He waved his hands back and forth, taking deep breaths, while shaking his head. The prickle under his skin began to subside, and his focus slowly returned.

He looked over to where he had dropped the lamp. The crest was a button? The lamp had some sort of deterrence built in. So, perhaps there was a cipher to this crest that prevented from triggering said deterrence. How very clever, Aladdin thought.

He reached for the lamp, and that was when the lamp jumped into the air, seemingly of its own accord.

From inside the vessel came a sharp, loud *ping* that repeated itself a second time. Then a third. With each *ping* the lamp jumped and spun in the air, until it became a rapid, sharp clatter, the lamp appearing to dance madly along the sand and brick. Aladdin stepped back as thin metallic extensions reached out from within the base. The lamp then righted itself on them.

Aladdin stepped back, his eyes narrowing on the metal plate now growing wider and wider. The metal was—beyond his reason and senses—stretching.

In fact, the lamp was growing *larger* before his eyes.

What was once a piece of metal easily carried in one hand had grown to half of Aladdin's size. The bulbous reservoir was now pulsating as would a man's chest when taking in great draws of air while the spout stretched and thickened, reaching down to the lid and balancing it just on top of the spout's opening. The handle snaked around what now appeared as a waist, and try as the golden sash might, the bands of metal sagged under the weight and girth of the growing belly. The arms were also creeping from the hole in this brass giant's back. Struts and coils of brass, gold, and silver intertwining like snakes around each other, taking on the look and texture of powerful arms. Aladdin swallowed nervously as the monster flexed its fingers, causing its sinews and muscles to move in concert with the digits. Considering the height of this beast was now well over twenty feet, those arms could easily squash Aladdin before he could move.

It stood tall, towering over him, and the pinging, grinding, and groaning. Silence returned, but only briefly.

Pop, and between the spout's mouth and the lid, a ball of flame appeared. The lamp's lid now looked like a tiny hat on this sphere. The polished surface of the lid and the massive body underneath it, cast light everywhere, making it slightly brighter in the cave.

Aladdin's eyes narrowed as it saw colour—no, details—in the ball of light. Two smaller fires danced and swirled where there would be eyes, and there was even a thin line of scarlet flame where he could easily imagine a—

"Oh dear," the line of fire surged and shimmered as it asked, "did I startle you?"

He felt the ground shake, but Aladdin's eyes never left the massive brass creature now looking down at him with glowing green eyes.

"Yes, that is the usual reaction I get." The thing took a step back, and gave a slight bow. "Forgive my rather theatrical introduction, sir, but how can I help you presently?"

Aladdin understood the thing. It was speaking in a perfectly civilized manner. He however was having problems. "What— what—what..."

"And there is the stutter," the creature muttered, shaking his head. "Let me try this again." He looked around and then gave a quick little nod at seeing a large, golden column; it would have been used as a pedestal for a small statue, or as a centrepiece in a court square. Apparently, this thing was using it as a walking stick. A free metallic hand reached up and tipped the lid on its fiery head. "Sir, many thanks for freeing me from the land. You may call me Giles."

That was when Aladdin saw it. The lid was no longer a lid. It was a bowler as the infidels wore—but made of brass. "Giles?" he finally stammered. "Giles the Genie?"

It nodded, giving a light shrug as it added, "Rather catchy, don't you think?"

Aladdin went to say something but hesitated. "Well, yes now that you think on it." He blinked. "A moment, if you please, but what exactly are you?!"

Giles placed his bowler back on his head. "I am the Genie of the Lamp."

"No, no, no, no!" Aladdin protested. This was not the way his mother's stories went. "You're supposed to be a great and powerful spirit imprisoned within an ordinary object. You're not supposed to be an automaton that pretended to be a lamp."

"And flying carpets are not supposed to be homemade ornithopters made up of clockwork gears and rug scraps, now are they?"

Aladdin blinked. "You...you saw that?"

"Of course I did!" Giles said, with a mechanical wink. "Just because I was in my state of concealment does not mean I am completely blind, deaf, and dumb to the world." For a moment, he loomed over Aladdin before picking up one of his legs and gently bending it. "Would you mind if we went for a walk? I would very much like to stretch the coils and struts, if you please."

He motioned deeper into the cavern, and Aladdin tried to keep up as best he could. Looking up at Giles, he could now see the large, gaping maw that was his back but inside it were wild collections of rods, gears, and boilers of all sizes and shapes. From here extended all the various workings that comprised of Giles' arms. The base that had grown to the size of a merchant's cart was now connected to the torso by a large, thick trunk, its point of connection covered by the coils that also doubled as the sash Aladdin had originally envisioned. He did not walk so much as floated as the base remained suspended above the sand and stone floor by a small space of æther.

"How do you know the stories?" Aladdin asked.

When Giles looked down at him, he was smiling. "My creator. A brilliant woman, she was. Not only did she construct me to serve as her valet, she also used me as her library for all her stories."

"All her stories?"

"All one thousand and one of them." He motioned with his massive walking stick to a large pile of gold coins. His trunk inclined and he now appeared to be sitting, using the mountain of fortune as a settee. "Much like the magical creature of my mistress' stories, I can enact amazing feats of wonder, but my magic is confined to some rules of the mechanical sciences."

Aladdin sat cross-legged at the foot of Giles, his head tilting to one side as he considered the automaton and its original size. "The rules of mechanical sciences?" he blurted out.

"*Some* of the rules," Giles stated. "There are certain things I do that science cannot explain; the cost of such magic is my own limitations to the sciences." He gave his walking stick a little twist into the gold underneath it and then motioned to Aladdin. "And there is, of course, my service, that my creator did make me swear an oath to. Therefore, I am at your disposal until you send me away."

Aladdin shook his head. "You are my servant?"

"I prefer the term valet. It sounds far more civilized, don't you think?"

Giles was a peculiar contraption, Aladdin thought quietly, but he did make him smile.

"For something buried in the sand," Aladdin said, looking up at the flickering face, "you certainly do not talk like a desert dweller."

"Again, a trait of my creator," he said. "She was inspired by some of the infidel explorers who touched upon our shores."

"Which explains your strange tongue," he added.

"One man's 'strange' is another man's refinement," Giles huffed with a visible jet of steam.

"You are no man."

Giles sat up straight on that, but then bowed his head to Aladdin. "This much is true." He went quiet for a moment. "And, sir, should I call you, sir, or should I refer you by another term?"

"'Sir' will suffice," Aladdin replied, not quite certain what to make of this odd situation.

"Then Sir, if I may be so bold, I may give you my thanks." Giles looked back in the direction they had come. "I was most relieved when you retrieved me from that other rather dodgy chap. I believe he would have employed me upon rather questionable pursuits."

Aladdin nodded. "I would agree. The man would have me believe he was my uncle."

"And he wasn't?"

"No." Aladdin felt a sudden pang well inside of him. He refused to think of it as a longing or regret; he instead dismissed it as hunger.

"The cad," Giles spat.

A growl from his stomach cut through the silence. Aladdin felt a heat rise in his cheeks, and he knew that it had nothing to do with the warmth coming from Giles.

"Oh dear, sir," the creature said, "I have been most derelict in my duties to you."

"What?" Aladdin asked. He suddenly grew aware that his hand was on his stomach. "What duties?"

"Forgive me, sir, but need I to look after you since you have freed me from my imprisonment."

"I don't think that is so great a service." Aladdin motioned around them. "How is this freedom?"

Giles raised a metallic finger and spoke in a calm, even tone. "I was imprisoned in my dormant form. I couldn't do much apart from keeping the shrine lit. Considering what talents my creator bestowed upon me, such a menial task is disappointing."

The valet's words seem to hang in the air around Aladdin. "What other things can you do?"

Giles stared at him with his green-fire eyes, and the flame that was his mouth curled into the most mischievous of grins. "Follow me, Sir."

Aladdin followed in the Giles' wake; the heavy, pearlescent fog lingering around his own ankles and eventually disappearing off into the treasures around him. He followed one of the wisps, the æther slinking across the ground serpent-like and then finding passage between a collection of goblets, bracelets, and other...

"Sir?" came the voice of Giles.

It sounded far off in the distance, but Aladdin nearly fell over as he was within an arm's reach of his automaton.

"You might want to walk to either my left or my right. Standing directly in my wake has a rather tranquilizing effect on organic matter."

Aladdin furrowed his brow. "Organic matter?"

Giles nodded and gave a light shrug of his massive brass shoulders. "My apologies. Bodies of flesh and muscle."

"Ah," Aladdin said, stepping clear of the mist and walking to Giles' right. He suddenly became aware of where they were walking. They were heading back to the sealed opening of the cave. He looked up at Giles now with new-found hope. His valet was tall. At least twenty feet tall. Perhaps thirty. This, along with the promise of talents yet seen, unsettled Aladdin as he felt the question tickling the tip of his tongue. "Giles, as you are such an amazing machine, why are you still here?"

The automaton chuckled lightly at the query. "Sir, did you not see? When I was left here in this vault, I had been left in a dormant state. My maker explained to me that her original intent faced corruption by those who would care to use me for ill ends."

"What sort of ill ends?"

"Think of what would happen if I fell into the hands of another tinker, or a band of tinkers charged with the shared goal of understanding how I worked. I would have been taken apart and then others would have been created. Soon, instead of being a creation of unique and original make, I would be part of a larger, formidable force."

That made Aladdin pause. He looked over Giles. "But you're a valet. A servant. What would you do—serve tea until the enemy submits?"

"Not quite." Giles brought up one of his arms and pointed it upward to the overhead hatch. "You will want to stay close to me."

The automaton thrust his arm forward, and Aladdin watched as his fingers and wrist slid backward. The digits that made up of his fingers locked into a forward position while braces rotated and locked into place. His arm went still and then his hand, which was now a ring of large, long barrels, began to spin. Faster and faster, until the hand and wrist were nothing more than a blur; and then jets of fire sprang from it, causing the vault ceiling to explode in rock and sand. Aladdin crouched, but knew he was safe at Giles' side as he continued to assault the area around a hatch. Even by plugging his ears with his fingers, the cannons' roar overwhelmed him, their thunder rattling his chest.

There was a moment's silence, and Aladdin finally dared to look up. He did this just at the moment when the desert surrendered to Giles' assault and the ceiling surrounding the hatch fell away, crashing into a large collection of gold coins, statues, and assorted gemstones.

"Now could you imagine the havoc an army of monsters such as I would wreck?" Giles asked.

Aladdin could only gape at the valet that apparently doubled as a war machine. His imagination easily pictured five such leviathans descending on Baghdad. He tried to conjure a Giles-model automaton army, and a shudder passed through him.

"Yes, my mistress wanted me to serve upon her, but defend myself as well. Then, as my skills sharpened, my ability to fend for myself evolved as well. She noted this, and therefore brought me here. She deactivated me, and put me to rest within the shrine, hidden amongst her husband's riches."

"You were hidden in plain sight?"

Giles nodded. "Like great illusionists, many disappearing acts are done with the object never leaving your sight. After her death, I watched as her husband searched the vault to his final day." He shook his head. "A cruel man who fell to his own infernal devices." The pensive look swirled and crackled, and then he looked at Aladdin with a pleasant smile. "Now, Sir, shall we tend to your hunger?"

Above them, sunlight poured into their cave. The exit still remained a good ten feet out of their reach; and there appeared to be no real leverage for them to manage escape.

"But, how?" Aladdin finally asked.

Giles looked up, then back to Aladdin and chuckled. "Oh, do forgive me, Sir. I lost my reason for a moment." He extended an arm—an arm that Aladdin recognized as one of the cannons Giles had used against the vault ceiling—and motioned with his other arm to a hatch that curved around his inside forearm. "If you please, Sir?"

The hatch opened of its own accord, revealing a small cage, just big enough for—

"You want me to get inside your arm?" Aladdin asked.

"Only for a small time," Giles assured him. "The space should accommodate you, perhaps not comfortably but adequately."

Aladdin looked into the compartment again and then back at Giles.

When his stomach growled, Aladdin knew there were no other options apart from staying in the vault and starving to death.

The cage groaned a bit as Aladdin pulled the door shut. "Pardon the squeaks. I will have that tended to, Sir." Giles then stepped under the open hole above them both. "Do hold on to the straps provided. This will be a bit bumpy, but a short flight nonetheless."

A short flight?

Aladdin's hands immediately shot for a pair of canvas loops as the cage around him began to shudder. Something was shaking Giles, or that was his first thought when he felt the metal clang and clatter against each other. He pressed his face against the cage's bans and watched wide-eyed as from underneath Giles' base a flower of flame blossomed and spread itself in every direction. His grip tightened on the straps overhead as he felt Giles' body shift upward. The treasure slipped out of view, the endless riches supplanted by curtains of sand and then finally the Persian desert in all directions. Aladdin could see through the bars the morning rays now touching the dunes, the endless black above his head now surrendering to hues of purple and blue.

Then he felt himself tip and Aladdin gave a cry of wonder and, perhaps, a touch of fear as Giles was now flying level with the ground. He was a massive creation and yet, somehow, the valet managed to stay in the air. Aladdin was high enough to tell they were moving at a great pace, far faster than he and Jaha did in their evening's long trek.

Giles began to tip upward, and from underneath them Aladdin heard the engine's roar angrily. Aladdin could see very little through the smoke and fire, but it was apparent that Giles was descending back to the desert. The odd sensation of flying, of floating above the earth ended abruptly, and Aladdin would have been knocked off his feet had he still not kept a strong grasp on the loop above his head. The engines underneath grew softer, and softer. There was only the sound of wind in his ears as Giles' arm lowered.

"There you are, Sir," Giles the Genie spoke cheerily as he undid the latch to his forearm. "I told you it would be a short flight."

Aladdin pulled himself free of the cage and looked around him. He was within a ten-minute walk of his home city. "Amazing."

His servant tipped his bowler. "Thank you, Sir. I hope you don't mind my saying, but yes, quite impressive considering how dormant I've been of late."

Aladdin let out a delighted laugh, but it faded into the growing sunlight of morning. "Giles, I do not think it would benefit either one of us if I walk into the city with you, being in the—" He motioned up and down the massive automation. "—form you are in now."

"Oh dear, Sir," Giles said, looking over himself. "I would wholeheartedly agree with you." The twin fires in his face winked out and then Aladdin heard the grinding of metal and gears again. Pipes and pistons were retracting, collapsing on themselves. Aladdin stepped back from the clatter and suddenly found himself in sunlight. That was when he noticed Giles' shadow.

Giles was getting…shorter?

The clamour began to settle and emerging from the steam and smoke was Giles, now eye-to-eye and in every proportion the same size as he.

With one noticeable difference, "How is this, Sir?" he squeaked.

Aladdin furrowed his brow, "What happened to your voice?"

"Well, Sir, with a larger body there are larger pipes and more voluminous spaces, giving my voice a deeper resonance and output. Reduce my size, passages are constricted, and there is very little for the sound to resonate from." He gave a shrug and smiled. "The science of acoustics, Sir."

And this marvel was his to command? "Giles, exactly what can you do?"

"Actually, Sir, I have yet to test my limitations in this form." He gave a bow and said, "Once I refill my boilers, perhaps we can discover them together?"

He nodded. A plan was forming in Aladdin's mind. "Yes, I believe we can. Tonight, perchance."

SIX

J aha was taking a deep bow at the ovation his illusion earned. He had, effectively, parted one of the Sultan's harem in half. Impressive, as it was one of his ladies and not someone directly under the influence of power of the All Powerful. Aladdin had to admit that.

What had he told him? *You hardly believe in such nonsense as magic, séances, and the like? A Frenchman named Robert-Houdin that opened my eyes at what many perceived as 'magic.'*

The boy took a deep breath. He would have one chance, one moment. He had to make certain it was the right moment. An eye-opening moment.

"And now, for my final trick of the evening," Jaha announced, raising his arms at the soft protestations—only an illusionist of his calibre could hush a Sultan. He then motioned to the ruler. "Tonight, though, I turn to you, Your Majesty, to assist me."

The Sultan clapped his hands. "Excellent. What is my part in your grand magic, All Powerful Jaha?"

He raised his hands and slowly pulled from his cabinet a pistol, one of the more modern ones no doubt brought from his European travels. The Sultan's guards immediately stepped forward, their hands working the bolts on their own antiquated rifles.

"Oh please, you believe the All Powerful Jaha would dare to assassinate me in a theatre full of people?" Aladdin watched as the Sultan parted the guards and slapped them both in turn. "If you did not kill him where he stood, I believe my people love me enough that they would tear him apart." Hefting his belly, the Sultan proceeded from where his harem and guards watched the performance and joined the magician on the stage, motioning for his subjects to rise. "Arise, my subjects, lest you miss the magic."

Over an uneasy laughter Jaha began, taking a step back while opening the chamber and presenting the weapon. "Your Majesty, I will ask of you to take aim at my heart and fire the pistol."

Another gasp and a few screams rose from the audience while the Sultan looked at the weapon with horror.

"Do not fear, Your Majesty. Do not fear," Jaha assured him. "I promise you the bullet will not reach me. Instead, I will catch it in mid-air, much like you have seen with Masters of the Far East."

"But…" the Sultan stammered, still looking at the pistol. Aladdin had never saw the Sultan sweat; an amazing feat from Jaha. "But the bullet…"

"Yes, I know," Jaha said with a charming smile, "but you must trust me and my skill."

Aladdin bit his bottom lip. *A Frenchman named Robert-Houdin that opened my eyes at what many perceived as 'magic.'* It was a matter of perception. He watched as Jaha loaded the weapon in front of the Sultan, his words explaining exactly what he needed the Sultan to do.

Somewhere in the midst of instruction, Aladdin took notice of Jaha's hands. It was a simple sleight of hand from the streets, the streets he knew all too well, but an eye such as his caught it. Jaha was palming something. Something small.

His eyes narrowed on the pistol, then went back to Jaha's hand. Could this magic truly be just as simple as a sleight of hand?

The Sultan nodded, swallowed and stepped to one side of the stage.

"And…" Jaha took in a deep breath and smiled. "Ready."

The pistol came up. It shook, and Aladdin was convinced the bullet was going to miss Jaha completely.

The pistol fired, causing some of the harem and a few ladies in the audience to faint. Jaha was frozen in a rather dramatic pose, and the expression on his face was not one of agony or fading strength. He opens his hand—the one Aladdin saw him palming a small object—and reveals to the Sultan and to the audience a bullet.

"Sir," the voice whispered from behind him. "I noted the Sultan's rather poor steadiness as well as the calibre of bullet that cad is presenting. Neither of them—"

"That is why it is an illusion, Giles," Aladdin whispered back. "And sadly, I think…"

"Brilliant!" the Sultan exploded. He then motioned to the people in the audience and to his own harem. "Arouse those who fainted. We must have an encore?"

Jaha gave a slight start. "Your Majesty?"

"There were those of my court and of my regime that missed this sorcery of yours, and I insist on an encore!"

Jaha spread his arms wide. "Indeed, Your Majesty, I am honoured, but I should have time to rest."

The Sultan's jubilance abated, and a darker expression passed across his face. "You will deny my wish, at this command performance?"

Aladdin now switched his gaze to Jaha, and the All Powerful magician was growing slightly pale.

It was only for a moment as he turned to the audience and asked in a broad, booming voice, "Shall you see this wonder again?" The theatre erupted into applause. "Very well then," he called over it. With a flourish of his robes, he turned back to the Sultan. "If you give me a moment, Your Majesty, I will prepare my pistol for you once more—"

"No need, All Powerful Jaha," the Sultan said, motioning to one of his guards. "My loyal guard are known across the empire for their accuracy. He will await on your command."

This was the moment. Aladdin gripped the backstage curtain. Timing would be crucial.

"Giles, the time has come."

His valet, the glow from his face cleverly shielded by extensions from his shoulders, looked over to Jaha, then back to Aladdin. "What shall I do?"

"We will enact what we have discussed, but to do so, we must protect Jaha?"

"Protect that cad, you mean?" he asked, his voice rising slightly.

Aladdin shushed him and glanced back over his shoulder. Jaha was busy building up the suspense. Either that, or he was stalling. Only seconds to go before the Sultan grew impatient.

"Without Jaha, this whole plot will be meaningless," Aladdin insisted.

From the stage, he heard the Sultan say, "Forgive me, All Powerful Jaha, but we *are* waiting."

Aladdin turned back to Giles. "Protect Jaha. Just for this moment."

His servant shook his head and then straightened up. "Very well, sir."

The *click-clack* of a rifle bolt turned his attention back to the stage. Jaha was standing there before the guard, his stance now very different from the earlier illusion. Aladdin, knowing Jaha as he did, had no doubt that the clever magician would have some sort of plan to fool or foil such a wrinkle as he found himself in. *The life that my false uncle wanted to show me,* he thought as the guard shouldered his weapon, was not much different from his present life in the street.

Jaha waited, his own gaze steely and focused, apparently focused on the guardsman's hand. He was watching for tells. He was looking for the precise moment to move.

The rifle fired. Jaha landed on one knee, his arms raised in some manner to block his chest; but on doing so, the magician appeared to slip. His arms inexplicably remained suspended above him.

"Well now," Giles comment. "Most intriguing."

"Now, it's our turn," Aladdin said, motioning for Giles to follow.

Aladdin and Giles walked out of concealment, on to the stage. There were murmurs of concern and confusion as he walked up to the struggling Jaha. The magician went still on seeing him, and Aladdin smiled and pulled back the loose fabric of the man's robes, revealing to the shock and disapproval of the audience metal gauntlets covering his forearm. He flicked his finger against one of them, allowing the light ring to echo in the near-quiet theatre. He then motioned to the space between Jaha and the rifleman, giving a light flourish with his hand.

There, suspended in the air, spinning like a child's toy, was the bullet. It was much larger than the one Jaha had "caught" with the Sultan, and it remained suspended in its flight, and Aladdin slowly waved his hands around it, showing no strings or any sort of restraints holding it back. He blew on the slug gently, and then wrapped his hand around it.

"Let me get this for you, Master," Aladdin spoke, his humble tone filling the entire space around them.

The bullet was still warm but slowed down in its spinning once he gripped it. Aladdin pulled, and he felt the resistance on the slug lesson. He glanced over to Giles and noted a small light in his left arm begin to dim, until finally the light went out and the bullet was in his hand. At the same time Jaha's arms were released by the unseen force that had held them fast.

Aladdin looked around at the audience, including the stunned, slack-jawed Sultan, and then looked at himself, still in the grubby, plain clothes of a street urchin. "Not what you expected, perhaps, in the saviour of the All Powerful Jaha?" He gave a nod to the crowd, and then bowed deeply to the Sultan. "My apologies."

As he crossed the stage, Giles' chest and legs opened and created a half cage that Aladdin stepped into and spread his arms wide. His clothes fluttered as if caught in a hard wind, and before the eyes of the audience the fabric around his legs shimmered into a brilliant blue, free of dirt and grime. Across his chest formed silk of a matching shade, the robes matching the style of Jaha's. His hair now swirled and groomed itself, and from the top of Giles' cage, a fine turban was woven and secured on his head.

The cage retracted, and Aladdin took centre stage with a flourish, saying "And now I stand before you, transformed."

The audience, led by the Sultan and his court, erupted into applause.

Aladdin turned to Jaha, and this time when facing the man's growing fury, did not flinch.

"You discovered the secret of the lamp," he seethed, his words heard only by Aladdin.

"I have, *uncle*," Aladdin returned, the title he bestowed on Jaha given a slight edge. "Now, allow me to show you what I have learned from it."

The din was dying down, and Aladdin stretched his hands out before him. "My valet here is a creation I have inherited, and unlike my peer—" Aladdin motioned to Jaha's gauntlets still in plain sight. "—I will not share the science within my magic, for we are in modern times, are we not?" He bowed to Giles and then outstretched his arms. He heard his servant turned away for a moment, then turn back and slipped Aladdin into a familiar accessory. "And we can not only create magic from that which we inherit—we can create magic ourselves."

Aladdin ran to the edge of the stage and leapt. The screams of alarm soon changed to cries of wonder and appreciation as the boy swooped up into the air, performing arcs and loops over the audience with his carpet ornithopter. The balcony patrons waved to Aladdin as he flew by them, and the Sultan was on his feet, overcome with elation as he landed gracefully on the stage.

"The magic is within our grasp," Aladdin said, his words overflowing with the exaltation and excitement of his flight. "We simply must dare to dream."

He turned just in time to see Jaha moving towards him, his gauntlet now behind his head, poised in an attack. The magician suddenly stopped, his arm trapped across his face. Giles advanced on them both, the light in his arm flaring as he glided past Aladdin and drew closer on Jaha.

"Sir, the moment you asked on me has passed. What will you have me do with this cad?"

Aladdin slipped his flying carpet off his back and considered the magician. "Master Jaha, you took me on a quest for a treasure of the ages. Instead, I discovered something for more valuable—my destiny. So I should thank you." He stepped behind his metallic valet and spoke, "Giles, send the All Powerful Jaha back where you came."

"Gladly, Sir," the automaton replied, and now his other hand came up.

A second light flared to life in his arm; and now bathed in the glow coming from Giles, the air distorted around the All Powerful Jaha. Jets of æther from the automaton's base swirled around Jaha like dust storms of the desert, enveloping him in a shroud that tore at the air around him. Jaha opened his mouth as if to scream, but no sound came. The light flared even brighter—then all went dark.

Jaha was gone.

"Now for my next trick." Giles turned to the Sultan, bowed, and asked, "Would you care for a spot of tea, Your Majesty?"

No one moved. No one spoke. There was only silence.

Until the Sultan gave a little chuckle, to which he added an enthusiastic bursts of clapping.

His harem joined in the applause—and then the audience. Aladdin motioned Giles over to his side, and together they took a bow.

"Great wizard," the Sultan asked from his throne, "what is your name?"

"I am Aladdin, Your Majesty," he said, bestowing obeisance to his ruler. "My valet, Giles."

"Your Majesty," Giles replied, mirroring Aladdin's gestures.

"Young Aladdin, I am impressed with your apparent marriage of magic and sciences. I would be most interested in discussing them with you. Would you consider being a guest at my palace?"

Aladdin felt his breath catch in his throat, not from the invitation—but from the veiled girl standing alongside the Sultan's throne. She was with the ruler, but she was set apart from the harem. Her dark gaze fixed on Aladdin, and it seemed to sparkle in the gaslight of the theatre. Aladdin felt a slight heat rise in his skin the longer she looked at him.

The Sultan looked at the girl, then back to Aladdin. "My daughter here has also voiced her interest in hearing of the sciences. I encourage such interests, so you would please not only the throne, but the daughter to the throne."

Aladdin smiled, his eyes jumping from the concealed beauty to the Sultan. "Your Majesty, I live to serve."

"It is settled then." He clapped his hands and stood, turning to the audience still struck by the unexpected conclusion of this command performance. "Good people, we thank you for your attendance tonight. Master Aladdin will not disappoint you, I'm sure, in his next performance here; but until then, heed his words and dream."

Following one final ovation, the audience dispersed, leaving Aladdin and his mechanical companion with the Sultan, his daughter, and his court.

You will find your destiny as he promises, but perhaps not in the fashion that you may imagine.

As soon as Aladdin could, he would call on his mother.

"Sir," Giles asked, "what shall we do now?"

"Once we reach the palace," Aladdin said, his eyes darting back to where the Sultan's daughter stood. She was still watching him. "I need you to assist me in modifying my ornithopter to accommodate two flyers."

"Two, Sir?"

Aladdin gave his valet a sly grin. "I can think of no better way to win a woman's heart better than a magic carpet ride. Can you?"

The Little Clockwork Mermaid

PIP BALLANTINE

I jammed the harpoon hard through the tentacle of the kraken. Ink and blood clouded the water around me, but I narrowed my eyes and pressed deeper.

Folk from the Above had this idea that the sea is peaceful; full of gently swaying kelp and fluttering shoals of fish. If any of them could see what really happens in Mother Ocean they would be most surprised.

Our dramas might look prettier to human eyes, but they are truly vicious.

The bright orange loop of muscle flipped around my waist and tightened immediately. With another jab of my weapon I convinced it to loosen a fraction, so that when I flicked my tail I was able to squirm free.

To the right of me, I saw Sabrina slice through another searching tentacle. Her body was almost obscured in the clouds of black ink and blue blood, but a quick echo-pulse told me where she was more precisely anyway.

Another rapid call, and I spotted Ondine swimming hard sunwards, ink trailing from her sides. She was escaping the cloud and the tentacles, and I hoped she was not injured.

"Lorelei," Sabrina cried, "get to the Hydra!" In the way of elder sisters, she was always reminding me of the blindingly obvious. It was apparent that we had achieved our mission, and that we'd provoked the kraken quite enough to lure it from its deep lair. It was time for the kind of speed that even our powerful tails could not provide.

Still, I waited until I could ascertain that Sabrina was coming too, and then I swam swiftly in the direction of the machine. This deep down the beautiful colours of my tail were dulled to greys and shadows, but as we angled sunwards the shimmering blues and greens became visible. I admit I was always vain about my tail. What mermaid isn't though?

With Sabrina close behind me, I saw the Hydra loom up pretty fast. The sleek, brass and steel machine resembled nothing so much a sharp–edged fish. Already four of my remaining elder sisters Tethys, Ondine, Nerissa and Ianthe were at their stations, clinging to four of the six control positions. They looked remarkably calm considering what was about to launch itself after us.

I quickly took my place, tucking my tail in tight against the Hydra, and locking my arms into the control glove.

Sabrina was in a similar position within heartbeats. Six sisters, six controls and six heads. My father was not without his little quirks, but family was everything to him, and he had made this machine for his girls.

Tethys, the eldest of my sisters, flicked her gaze over one shoulder. I didn't need to look—I knew the kraken was coming. I could feel him. Tethys was always the one who needed to be sure of every move she made—even when fleeing from a monster of the deep. Whatever she saw, was obviously quite enough even for her, as she shoved the accelerator chadburn upwards hard enough for me to worry she might have broken it.

The Hydra shot forward, powered by father's steam and magic engine. It was so rapid that we all closed our eyes and had to rely on echo-pulse alone. I could feel the Hydra shuddering beneath me, and for a moment I worried that the machine might fly apart under such stress. It was a new form of transport, and one I didn't think that Father had tested it at top speed.

Still, I had a job to do. I heard Nerissa on the other side of the machine working her propulsion jet, and I scrambled to keep up. The jets worked in tandem to propel us forward—my father's not so subtle commentary on how his girls should be.

My heart raced in my chest, but I knew now was the time. I pressed my body against the extending head of the machine, as I worked the controls to aim it.

The kraken was very much still in pursuit; its tentacles shooting out with all the strength of thrown spears, while the beast thrust water and jetted after our little fleeing family.

Still it might lose interest, so it was time to peak it a little.

The Hydra head I rode peeled away from the main frame and turned back in the direction we'd come. I couldn't see Nerissa's delight, but I was sure it couldn't be as amazing as my own.

The head was carved like a sea-snake's—and just as deadly. Twisting my right arm, I aimed it, and then with my left worked the tiny lever. The lever might be small but the effect was not. Five harpoons, tipped with steel and irritant poison from the stonefish, flew true, burying themselves in the thickest part of the arms of the kraken.

The monster didn't scream, but the nearby arms writhed madly. Now we really had its attention.

I chanced a look ahead and saw our target; the thick armoured hull of the human ship punctured the surface of the ocean, with its great paddles slapping the waves.

Ianthe, who was driving the front of the Hydra, bought us as racing up as close to the hull as possible. I grabbed tight on the head, and snapped it back into place against the main body of the machine; we were about to need all the speed we could get.

The sudden change in direction might have flung some of us off if we had not already been anticipating it.

The Hydra lurched suddenly downwards, diving towards the safety of the seafloor. I had only a moment to see the silver light of the mysterious moon on the water, only a second to think how good it would feel to break into the strange world, and then all was darkness once more.

The kraken had excellent sight, and could have turned easily to pursue us, but luckily the beast was also intensely territorial; the looming bulk of the human ship was taken by it as a more direct threat.

Its arms were already clamped on the underside of the ship, and I discerned immediately the groaning of iron and steel under assault. This was one vessel that would not be dropping depth charges on our cities again.

As Ianthe piloted the Hydra back home, none of us could contain our excitement. It was my first battle in defence of our world, and elation swelled in my chest and could not be contained. I began to sing.

Mermaids all sing for many different reasons; when finding an exquisite shell, when courting a husband, or for luring stupid sailors to their death. I sang a war song Father had taught me, and I sang it so well that none of my sisters joined in. I might be the youngest, but I had the talent of song from our syrienne mother.

Three dolphins appeared, looping and swimming around the Hydra, before eventually powering along beside me. The lead one I recognized by the chunk missing from his pectoral fin. Dolphin names were long, complicated and meant to be enunciated over extensive fishing expeditions, but they allowed us to shorten them. This one was young, and I had been able to choose his name Rive.

Fine water-voice, sister-daughter. Almost flash-fin though you ride the steel beast.

I smiled as I sang but did not rise to the bait. Flash-fin was what the dolphins called themselves in our language. Even us merfolk were not nearly as graceful and speedy as the whales and dolphins. They were full of disdain for the machines our father created, and they were the butt of many finned jokes.

Still they did not make jokes about my voice. Instead, the three of them kept easy pace with the Hydra as I sang. Rive and his pod circled and twirled about us, dancing to the rhythms of the victory song.

It was a pure moment where even my elder sister Tethys, smiled. I hoped she would keep that smile tomorrow when it would be my turn for venture Above.

Ianthe piloted the Hydra through another thick stand of kelp, and then we burst out into the soft sand plain that surrounded the city.

Every time I saw it, my heart gave a little leap, and then a little lurch. Its tall coral spires and brightly coloured waving seaweeds, were home—a beloved and blessed place. It was all I knew and that made it less than it could have been.

Ondine, nearest turned to me, and her dark green eyes flickered over my face. She was the next youngest sister after me, and our connection was the closest.

"Nearly home," her voice was pitched through the water to just me. "And tomorrow everything changes for you."

Only last year it had been her turn to travel Above and see what lay beyond our father's kingdom. She had returned almost frightened by it, and as far as I knew had never ventured there again. Still, she had not laboured the point with me—knowing how I yearned to see what she had—and I loved her for that care.

Ondine took great pains to soothe all around her that she could—even prickly Tethys.

I nodded in response but dared not speak. Instead, as the Hydra darted down towards the entrance to the coral palace, I sang louder, and this time a different song; this time the royal march; the song of our father and long dead mother.

Ianthe brought the Hydra to a stop before the periwinkle blue gates, and my sisters and I gave up our posts. Our father, Triton with his flowing grey locks of hair and muscular silver tail waited for us, hovering among the ranks of sea-guards. His smile was so large that I couldn't help giving one in return.

Even I yearned to make my father smile like that all the time. My heart swelled with pride as we swam up in line. The six marital sisters of the sea King—for once I was not ashamed to be one of them. For once I was just like the rest.

"My girls," Father said, embracing each of us in turn, "you have done a great thing today for the kingdom under the waves. So many have perished under the explosives of these vile human ships, but today you have struck a blow for us."

"Well, the kraken actually struck the blow," I whispered. Tethys shot me a look that could have come from a sea snake.

Father either did not hear or chose not to. "A well done task, and tomorrow Lorelei, it is your name-day, the day your mother, Ocean bless her, birthed you." His voice was full of pride and love, but his eyes could not meet mine. It was also the day our mother had died. None of us could get away from that fact.

Once he had collected himself, he flicked his tail until he hovered next to me. His hands clasped my shoulders and pulled me into a tight embrace. For a moment I let myself sink into it, softening my spine to his kindness—but it couldn't last long. As always the thin spectre of my mother came between us.

When he pulled back though I thought both of us had very respectable smiles on our lips. It was almost good enough to fool even myself.

"When you rise through the waves tomorrow," Father went on, angling his body so that all of my elder sisters were included, "you shall see many things. Nerissa saw a shipwreck from sunwards. Ondine witnessed a great river spill its banks and wash away a whole village into our kingdom, and Tethys," here he smiled on that blessed first, "she was brave enough to swim into the estuary and to the very shore of the evil city itself."

I had heard that story so many times that it took every ounce of willpower not to roll my eyes. Tethys was the unit of measurement for all us daughters of Triton. None had repeated her act of bravery...well none so far.

I had made no mention of my plans—even to Ondine—as I was sure every one of my sisters would tell our father. If that happened even custom would be set aside. King Triton of the waves would have none of his daughters do as I planned to do.

Every one of the merpeople in his city loved to talk about the beauty and grace of Queen Eleine—but none of them ever mentioned that she had been a syrienne. I had only learned this little secret from our paternal grandmother.

She had taken one too many weed-pods after Ondine's name-day celebrations, and let this little secret slip. It was why I had been practicing in secret. If Mother had been a syrienne, then buried in her daughter's blood, that power still lived. My sisters might not be happy to use it—but I would do everything I could to make home safe. Perhaps then Father would let us out of his sight...and into the bright world above and beyond.

The tradition of name-day ventures to the sun was ancient; as buried in myth as the city itself. Even my father as King could not disobey these traditions, since the clans of merfolk were fractious enough.

My mother the syrienne he had married because he wanted to seal that alliance, but after her death it had come a fragile thing. He might look at me out from under his eyebrows as bushy and wild as seaweed and glower, but he could not stop me.

With that realization lodged under my chest, I left the discussion of the battle to my sisters and swam into the palace. Tiny glow fish swam to and fro in the corridors, and their faint illumination was enough for merfolk to see by. The echo-sight led us through the dark and hidden places of our underwater home, but many clans preferred to see the beauty of the world; the flickering of the fish, the antics of the octopus, and the fluttering of the coral.

The palace was alive, as alive as the merfolk that lived in it. I liked that about it, and wondered if it was the same with the palaces of the human people. Did the sun produce beautiful plants as the ocean did? If they didn't have fish, then what animals did they have instead?

I yearned to find out.

I was so deep in contemplation that I nearly ran into Grandma. She was swimming down from the coral tower where all of us daughters of Triton had our quarters. Grandma was Father's mother, but had none of the traits of her son. That was lucky for me—if she had been as watchful and concerned as he was then I could not have gotten away with nearly as much as I did.

Her blue eyes widened as she literally bumped into me. I was beginning to suspect that Grandma's sight was not all she pretended it was and echo-sight was far too common for her to rely on. "Oh Lorelei, you gave me quite the fright! I didn't expect you home so soon."

"It wasn't a long mission," I replied, wrapping my tail around hers to prevent her from drifting away. Healthy merfolk could maintain a spot while conversing, but Grandma was getting to that point where she would not ask for help, but might need it.

She chose to ignore my slight, by pulling me into a hug as if that was what she had meant to do all the time. "Anytime you girls deal with the kraken I do worry. That old beastie is wilier than your father gives him credit for. Most especially today I did not want anything to go wrong." She snagged a passing glow-fish and dragged it closer to us. By its light she was able to examine every inch of me.

"Hmmmm," she mused. "I see a few cuts and scrapes, but nothing that can't be mended by a little overnight application of sillweed."

I shrugged but decided not to argue with her. Grandma knew her healing.

Taking my silence as complicity, she let go of the poor fish and grabbed me instead. It would have been impolite to struggle against her, so I swam in her wake as she guided me into the coral tower. Despite the fact that this had been my original destination, I was a little annoyed to be towed along like a sprat. In my own tiny room, Grandma had not been idle while her martial granddaughters had been away.

A wreath of sea-iris had been carefully plaited and lay spread on my clamshell bed, while hanging by the window was a length of glimmer-weed worked into a shift. Unlike humans, we merfolk did not need clothing at all—in fact it was generally thought of as reserved for the ill and the terribly aged. However, on special days such as tomorrow, exceptions were made.

"Oh Grandma!" I couldn't help myself, picking up what she had made and holding it up to myself. The glimmerweed had been artfully woven, so that the shimmer of the plant would wrap around my body, and not impede either my beauty or my tail. I wrapped my hair, dark and long like my mother's, around one fist and held it away from my neck.

"Oh no, no!" Grandma fussed. "Your hair is so beautiful; you must keep it down." She swam in a tight circle around me, demonstrating just how she thought my hair should be wrapped with the help of the wreath. Then she dragged me over to the polished piece of sea-glass, that one of father's artisans had cut and polished. "Lorelei, look how beautiful you are," she demanded.

I turned slightly from side to side and frowned. "I don't know why it is important that I be so dressed up. I am just seeing the sun and the Above after all."

"It's not just that," Grandma said with a wink. "Your mother was on her first trip sunward when she met your father. Perhaps you can do the same for yourself…"

I had learned not to roll my eyes in front of Grandma—she took exception to it—so I merely nodded demurely.

After an hour had passed, Grandma was convinced that I was only going to the surface to find myself a good husband, and not to see what the sun had to offer in any other way. My sisters arrived just as she was winding down. Ondine appeared at the doorway, her long turquoise tail flicking slowly back and forth, barely able to keep her upright.

"Oh Ondine!" Grandma turned her critical eye on my sister, "I hear you did very well today on your father's mission, but I really haven't heard you play your lyre today at all. We have a selkie prince coming in three days to sue for your hand, and it would be very nice if you could—"

"Grandma," Ondine held up the in demand hand. "I suffered a few wounds today, and I would like to rest. I think my playing can wait for another day."

I knew our Grandmother loved us and had spent her whole life caring for the daughters of her son, but she could take things a little too far. However, because I was reliant on her good graces to see the sun tomorrow, I could not go as far as my sister...at least for the moment.

"Yes, well," Grandma brushed off the dismissal, "you better rest then dear. As for you Lorelei, you best get your rest too. Tomorrow is an important day." Then with a flick of her tail she was gone—probably to check one my other four sisters.

Ondine smiled at me. "You better take her advice Lorelei...that beauty sleep might help you catch a husband tomorrow." She winked at me, and then flicked her way off to her own room. With a sigh I closed the door. My other sisters would have similar jabs to deliver...since I had been especially annoying when it had been their time to see the sun.

Over by my window, I leaned on my elbows and gazed out. Above the rays of daylight were filtering down on my father's kingdom, and it seemed impossible that when they rose again I would be there to see them on the surface of the water.

I was so nervous and excited that I really wondered if I could get to sleep, but the adventure today with the Kraken had been both exhilarating and tiring. I dragged myself over to the stack of nest weed wrapped in my shell and laid my tail down to rest. I didn't remember falling asleep but I must have, because before I knew it my sisters had charged into my room. The waters around the castle were still dark, but this was the ceremony that I had been waiting for my whole life—or at least it felt that way.

Ondine and Nerissa pulled me out of the nest weed before my tail even had time to catch up with what they were doing.

"Today's the day," all five of them were singing. "Our sister becomes sun kissed."

Their voices twined together and I would have joined them, since I was bursting with happiness, but it was not the tradition. So I allowed myself to pushed and pulled into the outfit Grandma had created. They spun me about, laughing in front of the sea glass mirror, and I realized that they were right. I was ready.

Then in a tumult of song and laughter they pulled me down the stairs of the tower and out into the courtyard.

These were our sea gardens, populated by the most beautiful plants and creatures of our father's realm. Silvery starfish gleamed in Ianthe's garden, and she plucked them up and arranged them in my hair. Tethys had a string of seashells in bright pinks and purples, which she had strung into a little bracelet, which she put on my wrist. I felt more beautiful and cared for than I had in all my life.

Then my sisters spun me around and pushed me out the door and into the castle, to emerge into the splendour that waited. The front of the palace gleamed with fish lights that circled the turrets and trailed along around those assembled there. Every clan of the sea was there; syriennes, triskies, selkie, and a plethora of other clans that I had no time to appreciate, as my sisters were dragging me over to where our father and grandmother waited.

Father was wearing his crown of coral and shark teeth, while Grandma was wrapped in a cloak of whale shark that I knew had belonged to my grandfather. Unlike my sisters, they were not laughing. In fact, Grandma looked distressed. Perhaps the joy of yesterday had been put on for my benefit. I suddenly felt bad about that.

Father was leaning on his trident; a mighty thing that had been part of the royal insignia since before written records. I had heard the rumour that it had been taken from a human god in the last battle of Land and Sea. It gleamed with many different strands of metal, and was wrapped in a kind of light that did not seem to need the sun.

"Daughter," Father said, his voice heavy with sadness, "this is your name-day. You have passed the eighteen years required to become a martial princess in name, and you have proved your worth in an under the water battle. Today, you must journey towards the sun and see the fight that lies there. When you return, you will know your place."

He put his hands on my shoulders, and I felt for the first time the edge of the sadness that he was feeling. Grandma leaned forward and kissed my cheek.

She whispered into my ear, "Be great, Lorelei, but also be wise."

Her eyes when she looked into mine were strangely hard—as if she could see something I could not.

Still, this was the day I had been waiting for since I knew of it, and I wasn't about to let my elders' sombre attitude reach me. When Father released his hands I was away and didn't look back.

I flicked my tail hard and angled my body upward, a huge grin already on my mouth. As I went I heard the gathering start to sing, but I was soon away from them. My eyes were locked on the darkness above—to the place I knew the sun would come first. My sisters followed my ascent for a little while, keeping pace with me, but as I began to feel the pull of the surf, they dropped away below. The final notes of their song died away behind me. Ondine was the last to leave me. Her clear, green eyes locked with mine. "Do not look too long Lorelei. The sun can burn," she whispered.

And then she was gone, and it was—finally and completely—my experience. As I swam the last hundred feet upward, it suddenly occurred to me; this was not merely the first time I would see the Above world, it was also the first time I had ever truly been alone. As a princess of Triton, I had always been surrounded by sisters, family and sycophants.

Yet, in this moment I was just Lorelei, experiencing something for herself.

I was so busy thinking on that that I crested the waves and broke water without slowing down. I breached the waves like a dolphin, flying through the air for a second of strange and beautiful unintended acrobatics, before landing with a splash in the surf. I bobbed there, taking my bearings and regaining my breath. I was in fact breathing air. It felt very odd on the exposed gills on my throat.

It took some getting used to, but as long as I kept my gills damp I could manage for a while. Around me was darkness, which usually would not have been a problem, but my eyes were used to the depths of the ocean, and nothing seemed as it was. I was as a human in this world. In the near distance I could make out a looming shape, which had to be the island where the humans lived. The tide was pulling me in there, and I did not resist it.

I let it take me. I rolled over and floated on my back contemplating that wonder of wonders, the sky. The sun was coming. Beams of red light washed through my hair and made me blink. I flipped quickly over into the water, cresting it, and bobbing like a piece of flotsam among the waves.

I had waited so long for this moment; I was going to enjoy every little bit of it. The clouds on the horizon were not playing fair; hiding the full glory of the sun. That was probably a good thing, since I had been warned not to stare directly at the dawn—but I was completely ignoring that advice.

As the streams of pure golden light punctuated the layers of clouds and sent them dashing across the surface of the water, I was in awe. This was true power. The sun ruled the sky, but also was great enough to touch my father's kingdom beneath the waves.

After daylight had taken over, my mind was satisfied…at least in one respect. It was not just about seeing the sunrise—it was also about understanding the Above world. I was a martial princess after all, with the heritage of Triton and my syrienne mother.

So, I turned myself towards the distant shore and dived a few feet beneath the ocean. Swimming like a dolphin meant feeling the euphoria they did, as I made my way closer and closer to this strange thing called land.

I had been cautioned by my sisters not to be seen by the men of the Above. Since our battles with them, any merfolk caught would be captured and strung up like a fish for display.

So it was with a racing heart, and a shiver of delicious fear down my back, that I approached the harbour. Carefully, I stayed back from the breaking waves and kept only my eyes and the top of my head out in the dry world. Humans did not have very good eyesight really, and they would probably only see seaweed or debris floating in the water.

However, this early in the morning there were not that many of them about.

With wide eyes I saw some of the things that my sisters had whispered about; a city made of white stone on a hill leading down to the bay, and a river that curled its way past it to Mother Ocean. I could taste that river; full of dirt, and the remains of plants. It carried both the dead and the living alike. Ondine had actually dared to swim up the river a bit since it was wide and deep. The things she had seen there—strange creatures, trees that scraped the sky, and mountains that dominated the interior of the island.

I found those interesting enough—but not as interesting as people; people who had legs instead of tails and breathed air instead of water. I watched from the waves, seeing narrow plumes of burning fires smudging the sky. Father had told us about the industry of Above folk; how they folded metal and bent it to their will. That was why he had taken to tinkering himself. The ships of the humans were desecrating our world, and he want to make sure that the merfolk were not left behind. In fact, the Hydra was a modified human design.

The trek to the sun was an ancient ceremony of my people, but Father had turned it to something else; a reconnaissance journey to judge the strength of the enemy. I did not need to look far to see that power.

Many ships stood ready in the harbour, and only two of them were simple fishing vessels. The others were vessels of war with cannon, and metal slides for dropping depth charges. I dared to swim closer to the pier, until I was beneath one of these massive creations. This was one that had sides of iron and smelt dangerous.

My mind was finally getting over the newness of the situation, and now I could look at the ships with a more critical eye. This one had portholes for its armaments—we had seen those for generations—but the cannon posed no threat to merfolk, they were for ship-to-ship battles. I flicked my tail and circled to the rear of the vessel.

My breath caught, as I observed a long slide at the rear and knew immediately what they were for. Depth charges were only aimed at the merfolk. They would kill our people and destroy our cities.

This sight somehow made me sick of the Above world, and I was about to turn tail to return to my father's kingdom—but then my eye was caught by movement up on deck.

A young man stepped out from one of the cabins, with a pistol in one hand, and a spyglass in the other. He had long dark hair, and was dressed in the uniform of Above folk that my sisters had told me about. Most of all, he had legs. My eyes were riveted to those amazing appendages, and how they worked in tandem as he strode to the railing of the ship. I slid in closer to the hull so he might not see me, but I could observe him.

That was when one of the ships moving into the harbour opened its gun ports and began to fire. I had observed it, but hadn't been able to tell it was any different from the ships already at anchor.

I ducked instinctively into the water, flicking my tail to take me deeper. The pressure of the explosion above me ran all along my body. Red light burned my eyes as debris began to impact on the water and slowly tumble towards me. The ship was now a tilting wreck entering my world.

I felt my heart leap into my throat, but it was moving in slow motion, and I was much faster beneath than above. I flicked, dived, ducked, and got out of the way. So many strange objects were falling, but there was one I recognised; a human shape in a dark.

I didn't even notice that I was moving, until I had him in my arms. He was heavy, but I was strong. My tail flexed and bent, as I angled us towards the surface but some way from the destruction at the port.

We broke from the water abruptly, and the light of the burning ship was hard on my face as I swam him away from the danger. I didn't know how hurt he was, and how much water he had swallowed. I had no idea just how much water one of his kind could take down and survive.

His head was draped against my shoulder, and I wrapped one hand against his cheek to hold him there. It was an awkward swim, but eventually together we flopped onto the soft sand of the far beach. I glanced up the cliff a little and saw a low structure there, but I wasn't sure if I should call for help from there. Would they even be able to understand me?

As we rocked back and forward in the surf with the burning ships lighting up the sky, I turned him over. His eyes were closed, and his dark hair was plastered to his skin like seaweed. I leaned in close to him, and laid my head on his chest. For a moment I thought there was no sound there, but then very faintly I heard it—the thump thump of a human heart.

He was beautiful. I realised that as soon as I raised my head. It was the kind of beauty I had not ever seen in my father's kingdom. Despite it being rather rude, I couldn't help but stare at his legs. It took me awhile to notice that his eyes were open, and he was staring at me.

They were a dark blue—even in this light I could tell that. They were unfocused, darting around my face uncertainly. "You…you saved me…" he muttered, his voice low and delicious. His eyes darted back and forward before his eyelids fluttered close.

I panicked for an instant, but his heart still beat in his chest. I smoothed his hair back from his forehead, and wondered at what his life must be like; birds flying overhead, air in his chest rather than water, and legs to propel him. The idea of that lodged in my head, like a sharp, beautiful piece of coral.

That was the exact moment that I heard the women's voices. Reflexively, I jerked back in the water as several cloaked figures came running along a path leading down from the cliffs. However, my fingers trailed reluctantly along the man's arms. I didn't want to let go—but there was nothing else to be done.

"Prince Roan," they called, but I was not there to see their arrival. By the time they had reached the beach, I had already wriggled my tail, and slid back into the embrace of Mother Ocean.

I didn't want to see any more of the Above world. I swam back to my father's kingdom with a sharp sensation in my chest that I could not name. My sisters, who had been waiting for me below the waves, fell in behind me as I wordlessly passed them heading deeper. I knew what they were thinking; I was disappointed or scared by what I had seen. They loved me—but they didn't really know me. I barely knew myself at that moment.

After the shock had worn off, and as I reached King Triton's kingdom once more, what I was contemplating was something I could not share with them. I was thinking about what stood between me and seeing the man I'd rescued again. For the next few days I said very little, but everyone—even my grandmother—left me alone to sort out my feelings. They thought I was stunned by the horror of what I had seen. I was only seeing the beauty replayed over and over again in my head.

I knew what I needed to do on the very first day, but it took me much longer to work out how I was going to achieve it.

My grandmother and father I spotted talking to each other quietly in the corners of the palace—watching me as covertly as they could. When they did that I smiled and slapped on the appearance of happiness. It wouldn't do to have them put guards on me—not when I had a person to visit. A person I knew they would most definitely forbid me from going to.

My mother had been a syrienne and like most of that kind beautiful and fierce. She had though wanted more than her kin could provide. That secretive tribe lived in the shadowy trenches from where monsters came, but they were also masters of making and creation. They would have the answers I sought, but I knew of only one syrienne who would not kill me on sight; my maternal grandmother—the one that was called the Sea Witch.

I told no one about my plan, because to do so would result in Father locking me up immediately. Instead, I waited until the darkest moonless night and stole away from my room like a thief. I took nothing with me: no gold, and no pearls. I was throwing myself on the mercy of the witch, and the frail hope that blood meant something to her. She had no interest in finery or fripperies from what I had heard.

Once beyond the walls of the palace, my tail powered me deeper and deeper, until sight was lost to me, and only my plaintive calls allowed me to keep following the trench.

Until, out of the darkness I saw a faint golden gleam and felt the hint of warmth on my skin. The Sea Witch's fortress was perched like a malevolent barnacle on the final ledge of the cliff, before the long uninterrupted plunge down. I could feel rather than see it; like a faint tremble on my scales.

The door to the fortress was a hatch, and my fingers told me immediately this was neither coral nor rock. Somehow it was made of all metal. Smelting ore beneath the ocean was a difficult undertaking, and this much of it was more than my father could have dreamed of having.

I turned the hatchway, flinching slightly as it ground open with a low groan. It didn't matter. I had no doubt that the Sea Witch, my darling grandmother, had known I was approaching long before I even touched her door.

Her glowing eyes were already fixed steadily on the entrance by the time I levered it open. No one knew her name—even I didn't, and I was related to her. She was simply the Sea Witch and feared as such. I hovered there on the threshold and took her in with a pounding heart.

Her face was as white as all creatures of the deepest dark with eyes that burned yellow, while her tail was the kind of black that disappeared into the shadows. However, it was her curved and pointed teeth that were revealed in a terrifying smile that I could not keep my eyes from. Her voice came at me like an unexpected harpoon. "Granddaughter, I have been expecting you for days."

I managed to repress a shiver, since I did not want to let her know how her use of the word terrified me. Suddenly my father's mother seemed as welcoming as gentle seaweed. How this creature had produced a daughter lovely and kind enough to entrance my father was a mystery—one that I was not going to ask about.

I cleared my throat, painfully aware of how my gills were trembling more than usual against my skin. "I have come to ask a boon—"

"Do not waste my time using your father's words." Her eyes narrowed on me. "Tell me what you really want and quickly!"

"I want a man of the surface world," I blurted out, completely caught unawares by my own boldness. Had she somehow forced those words out of me, from my own inner depths?

My other grandmother would have fainted, but this one merely inclined her head. "Still a better choice than your mother made."

I managed to cram back a defence of my father, and watched as she swam up towards the ceiling of her strange iron home. It took me a moment to realize that she had a surface! Through the geometry of the building, she had managed to trap a portion of air in the top section. I followed her instinctively.

We surfaced together, and I heard a faint thumping noise, which momentarily distracted me from the curve of her workbench covered with all sorts of delights.

"A small pump keeps the air from going stale," the Sea Witch commented, before gesturing me over to a section of her table.

Immediately nothing else mattered to me. My heart was racing as I looked at a pair of gleaming brass legs that lay there. I ran my eyes over the exquisite workmanship in them. The shape was made with hundreds, if not thousands of overlapping scales, that nonetheless formed the shape of the thing I desired most. I jerked my head to the right and peered down. Yes, indeed they were hollow in the middle, and thus meant to be worn.

When I stared up at the Sea Witch, I almost couldn't choke out the words. "Are...are they for me?"

Her smile was, I thought, meant to be kind. "I felt it in the deep currents that my blood was looking beyond the water for its purpose. I have been working on these legs for many moons now, but I never imagined they would be for you in particular…just for one of my daughter's girl."

I didn't even think why she would have made me such a thing. Instead, I darted forward, wrapping my fingers around them, but her freezing cold hand pulled me back by my shoulder. I sucked in a huge breath, as my syrienne grandmother grasped me under the chin and examined me. She turned my head from side to side, as if deciding how much of her own self was in me. It was hard to tell exactly what she thought because not once piece of her expression changed.

She produced a vial of black liquid that was contained in a clear whelk shell, and sealed with some kind of wax. "Before you put on the legs you must drink this." When I made to reach for it, she snatched it back and waggled her finger. "You must understand several things, granddaughter. The clockwork legs will split your tail within their workings, so the pain will be constant and excruciating."

I nodded but didn't say anything. I did not fear pain, but I did fear days of never ending sameness and just being another daughter of Triton.

"And then there is the potion," she said softly. "It will allow your tail to transform, and give you lungs instead of gills, but it will also steal your voice, forever."

By the way she paused, I knew she was ready for me to turn tail and swim away. Instead, I looked her full in the eyes when I spoke. "What is the point of being able to sing, if there is no one who understands me to hear?"

A flicker of something that might have been sorrow passed over her face. "Sacrifices must be made to get what you want. The question is, do you have the will required?"

I stared down at my hands for a moment, at the webbing between my fingers, and thought of what I would be giving up. My family would still be my family, but it would be different, and I would never be able to visit my father's kingdom again. Once I accepted that, I thought on deeper things; how I had never felt right at home like my sisters did. I'd always fought the feeling that I wasn't in the right place. If I turned away now I would be condemning myself to a lifetime of that, while Above there was the man with the beautiful eyes. And hope.

On a surge of fear, I grabbed once more for the legs, ready to pull them into the water and do the thing right there. The Sea Witch stopped me again, but this time a little more gently. "Not here," she said, "the legs cannot survive in water. I will wrap them for you and you must take them Above." She placed her hands on the knee joint, and with a flick of her fingers released a pair of brass keys that were imbedded there. "One important thing; you must make sure to keep them wound, and they will give you the freedom of the Above."

As she turned to wrap the legs, I stopped her by laying one hand on hers. "Why did you really do this?" I asked, determined that at least I should know my feared grandmother's reasoning for making such a thing.

The Sea Witch had her back to me, her short, pale hair plastered to her skull, the dripping of water down her back was so strange, but somehow I kept my eyes fixed on it. "I did not know they would be for you, but I have had the idea for them for years. If your father is ever to keep the Underwave kingdom safe, then we may need soldiers that can go Above."

It was a pretty—if disturbing story—and I wasn't sure if I quite believed it. The syriennes and the Sea Witch in particular had never shown much interest in protecting our world. Instead I imagined conquest might be her real reasoning.

It should have stopped me, but I considered that if I took the prototype, it might stop her. That and I could warn my prince if it looked like my suspicions might be justified.

The Sea Witch finished stuffing the legs inside a long, clear seaweed pod. She sealed the end of the pocket with a little burning implement, and pushed the whole bundle into the water close to me. Then, she pressed the bottle into my hand.

For a moment we looked at each other, and then she sighed. "Like your mother I see, for all the good and bad it will bring you."

Then, without further explanation, the Sea Witch ejected me from her house, leaving me clutching the pod with the legs in one hand.

I hovered there for a long moment, outside the iron door, clutching the thing she had made.

My brain was spinning, but I knew one thing—I could not dare go back to the castle. If my father found these legs he would know immediately that they came from her, and would dispose of them accordingly. Also, lingering in the back of my mind was the understanding, that if I went back, saw the faces of my other grandmother and my sisters, I might never do anything at all.

So I turned my own face upwards, already grasping the pod, but then I stopped—just for a moment hovering between the Above and the below. The Sea Witch was watching me with nary a sign of what she was thinking. On impulse, I leaned forward and planted a kiss on her freezing cold cheek. "Thank you, grandmother," I whispered into her ear. "Thank you for everything."

Then before she could say anything and spoil the moment, I flicked my tail hard and began to swim to the Above. I let the tides and currents of Mother Ocean lead me back to where I had seen my prince. When I surfaced, gasping and wide-eyed, it was luckily night. The stars seemed to me to be sparkling extremely brightly, and the moon a gleamed like a pearl in the black. With a smile on my face, I swam to the shore and beached myself as far as the waves could get me.

I lay there, looking up at the night sky, enjoying for one last moment my gills, and my tail. Then, I began to sing. It was the only memory I had of my mother. She had died shortly after my birth, so perhaps my recollection of the song as hers was not possible…but it was all I had of her. The song filled me and gave me strength. However, it couldn't last forever.

As the last notes died in my throat, I pulled open the vial of oily liquid that my syrienne grandmother had given me and downed the whole thing before I could give into fear.

The effect was immediate and terrifying. I felt as though I had swallowed a bag of knives. I would have screamed, but my throat was suddenly swollen and unable to let even a squeak past. As I rolled in agony on the smooth sand, some small, sane part of me knew I didn't have much time. With numb and fumbling fingers, I managed to tear open the seaweed pod. The legs were so very heavy, but I jerked them out with my shaking hands, and without thought jammed my beautiful, iridescent tail into the opening.

There was no more Lorelei, there was only the exquisite dance of pain in my nerves. The specks of stars darkened and fell in my consciousness, as the combined weight of the potion and my grandmother's device tore my tail apart. It tore me apart and scattered me on the ocean and the shore.

Eventually and miraculously, I came back to myself. I lay on the sand for a while and felt the pain subside. As my grandmother had warned, it did not go away entirely, but after the utter agony that I had suffered it actually felt good. As the dawn began to make itself known on the horizon, I finally levered myself upright and looked down.

I had legs—legs of gleaming brass. I flexed them experimentally, and they moved to my command. Through the pain a slow smile flickered on my lips. I couldn't wait, I pulled myself upright. My head swam at the sudden elevation, but the Sea Witch's device seemed to know what it was doing. I did not fall down, instead I staggered a few cautious steps.

However, there was something that the Sea Witch had not warned me about, something that made my heart ache; the legs made music when they moved. It was the faint clicking music that I had last heard when my sister had brought home a music box she had found floating after a shipwreck. It sounded so much better and prettier in the world of the Above.

I pulled my dark hair down over my shoulders, glad at least that it was still so long that it would provide some coverage. Humans, I knew were very strange about obscuring their naked bodies.

I turned myself towards the palace on the hill, and soon I found I was running towards it. It was not the speed that my tail had once been able to give me, but it was nonetheless exhilarating. The music of the legs surrounded me, and announced my arrival long before I got there.

My father had spent a great deal of time telling me about the cruelty of humans, but none of it had really sunk in…or perhaps it had been washed away in the eyes of my prince.

Women were running towards me now, perhaps thinking I was in distress, being naked and wearing brass legs and all. They couldn't possibly know that I was crying tears of joy not ones of fear. After the pain of the transformation I was incredibly brave.

I was an object of surprise to them naturally, but they did not hurt me. Instead, I was wrapped hastily in blankets and brought inside. All I took in straight away was the smells, but it wasn't as if I could name any of them. The huddle of women were asking me a barrage of questions that I couldn't have answered quickly enough even if I had my voice. They had a particular smell that I had nothing to base on, so I couldn't decide if it was good or not. I decided to think of it as pleasant.

They hustled me upstairs to the palace, and in the way of humans quickly had me wrapped in their clothing. It was the first time I had worn anything so covering, but I tried my best not to let it show.

Finally, the woman stood around me and slowed down with their questions. One in particular, with long, red hair like my sister Nerissa peered down at me, head tilted, examining my legs, or what of them could be seen under my skirts. Nervously, I slid my hand against my knee, and wound the key so that I would not be caught short if I needed to run.

"What is your name?" the girl said, slowly and loudly as if I was deaf.

I mimed the fact that I had no voice, even as my grandmother's device played on merrily.

The women exchanged surprised glances, but before they could ask anything else a loud voice called out. "Make way! Make way for the King!"

A barrel-chested man with grey hair soon had the women scattering before him. It was indeed the King of the Above. Even without the herald it would have been apparent from his bearing and the narrow band of gold he wore on his head. Surprisingly, he did not look that different than my own father.

The tiny, nervous fish fluttered in my stomach as he approached.

He examined me with a hard eye and then my legs even closer. When I mimed my lack of voice again, he had me open my mouth and looked down my throat. I wasn't sure what he was thinking he would find.

"I do not think this girl is much of a spy," he muttered. "More like some strange experiment escaped from a mad tinker. Not the first we have seen either." He dismissed me by simply turning and walking off.

Apparently that was all that was needed to make my arrival all right. The ladies descended on me once more, like I was some exotic pet, and swept me into their world.

For the first few days I did not see my prince, but I did see a lot of his sister. I found out, the girl with the red hair was Princess Iria, and she made me her project of the moment. I knew all about bored princesses and the things they did to amuse themselves.

Perhaps it was my silence, perhaps it was the marvel of my legs, but either way she kept me company. She also kept up a constant stream of conversation, most of which washed over my like warm waves and departed imparting nothing. However, sometimes there were pearls in the rocks.

I actually learned a lot in those first days, probably more than I would have had I had my voice. Listening bought me a lot of information—so much that if I had been a spy I would have discovered much from the stream of conversation Iria sent my way. It made a welcome distraction from the constant grind of pain that my grandmother's device provided. Once I had largely forgotten the agony of the potion, it remained ever present.

It was all made worth it when Prince Roan came on the third day. He burst into Iria's parlour without being announced and stood in the square of late afternoon sun like a jewelled fish of the reef. His eyes were as I remembered them, but he seemed even more desirable now in his own element.

The music of my legs grew louder when I saw him, but he took no notice of me. I might as well have been part of the furniture. "I found her," he proclaimed loudly and my heart leapt. Maybe he had noticed me!

Being wrong had never stung so badly. He was not looking at me.

"Roan, you're so rude!" Iria snapped, her hand dropping protectively down over mine. She must have thought the sudden tears in my eyes were due to his rudeness, when in fact they were due to the fact he didn't recognize me immediately. I thought I had made an impression when I saved him.

It got worse. "I found the girl who rescued me." I stared at him in horror, unable to move, as he told his sister excitedly how he had found the one girl that had fished him from Mother Ocean. Prince Roan went on at great length about her beauty, her kindness, and her strength. I knew one thing though, he was a fool and she was a liar.

Apparently he had found one of the girls who had come down from the temple, one that had rolled him over and dragged him out after I had returned to Mother Ocean. It was she that was taking advantage of my rescue efforts. If I had not caught him and dragged him Above he would be dead.

I should have been angry perhaps, but I felt as carved out as an empty whelk shell. Finally, when he was done, he turned to Iria. "And who is this, sister?"

The princess gestured to me. "Some poor simple child, a reject of one of those mad tinkers, father thinks. She has no voice at all, but her legs are quite remarkable."

With a surge of energy, I got to my brass feet. My mouth opened and I struggled to squeeze out words; the words that would tell him he'd been mistaken; it had been me there. I wanted to yell about how his head had rested on my shoulder, and how I had seen him standing on the deck of the ship before the attack. My throat choked up, burning with effort, but producing nothing.

Instead, it was my legs that spoke. The chiming rattle of the music box filled the room, and on its wings I began to dance. While Iria and Roan stood there, with wide eyes, I twirled and danced in the princess' parlour. I was desperate to communicate in whatever way I could.

It felt strange after dancing in my father's kingdom with my tail, but it pushed back the pain to the edges of my mind. After a while it began to feel very good. I hoped my dance would tell the prince it was me. I wished it contained my longing and hopes that he could understand as easily as words.

After a few minutes, when the music and the dance faded, Roan looked bemused rather than informed. "It is a lovely dance," he said, with a slight frown. He shrugged at his sister. "Your charge has quite the talent, sister. The gods have obviously seen fit to give her talent to make up for her deficiencies."

I thought the black potion had been painful, but the prince's blindness cut even deeper.

I did not give up. I couldn't. For Prince Roan was what I had given up Mother Ocean, my father, and all of my sisters for.

I became the prince's shadow. I trailed around behind him, and tried my best to reach him in the only way I could. At first he was kind, smiling when I began my little dances in every corner of the palace. I could not speak, and I could not write their language either—so the dancing was all I had.

After a week, he did not stop to watch. I danced desperately, even as I heard that this girl he had mistaken for me was coming to the palace. Roan's delight, turned to amusement, then boredom, and finally anger. Now he stalked angrily past me as I began to spin, and I realized I had gone too far. It was done. By trying to tell him so often, I had made myself abhorrent to the prince, and now even if the truth came out he wouldn't look at me with love.

However, I had one last thing to say.

The morning that the girl was to arrive, I waited outside his bedroom, and when he appeared, launched into a spinning, melancholy dance. I swept my arms and legs in long arcs, mimicking the broadness of Mother Ocean, and with smaller appealing gestures I tried to show him that I was sorry. I just wanted to be back in that moment where I had held him on the shore. I was no longer Triton's martial daughter. Somewhere along the way I had lost that.

He glared at me, and then turned away with a growl. "Idiot girl, Iria shouldn't just let you run around loose." And then he walked away.

Roan didn't see me. I watched, the syrienne's devices sending jolts of pain up my spine, as he went down the steps to meet the thin girl who only had dark hair in common with me. I had come here with such hope for something new, and all I had found was pain and loneliness.

I ran. I couldn't bear to see him welcome her, love her when he should have loved me. My father had been right after all; humans were cruel. Blindly, I made my way to the beach, my legs playing a sad tune that seemed to tell me nothing was worth this agony. The physical pain meant little.

I stood at the edge of Mother Ocean, and looked out over it, tears burning down my cheeks, and broken screams in my chest. The Sea Witch had said I couldn't return, and yet I wanted to. Death might await me in the sea, but I would be free of the pain, and I would get to see my family for a brief moment.

"Lorelei," a voice called, and it had been so long since anyone had spoken my name for a moment I wondered if I had imagined it.

I was even more surprised when I saw the dark shape of my syrienne grandmother lying in the surf. Whereas in the deep valley she had been rather terrifying, at the very edge of the Above she seemed smaller and vulnerable.

With the legs she had made sending shots of agony up my spine, I went to her, and slid down to sit next to her on the sand. I looked jealously at her tail shifting back and forth in the waves.

"This isn't how you imagined it, is it?" the Sea Witch said. When I shook my head, she nodded slowly. "Your sisters saw you walking up on the cliff face, and they could tell you were unhappy. It was Tethys who sought me out."

Fresh tears poured from my eyes, knowing that my sisters had risked much to find me, and loved me enough to do so. Seeking out our grandmother was something I never would have imagined from my stern older sister.

The Sea Witch touched my arm, drawing my attention. "I lied to you, granddaughter. I did not make the legs to make soldiers. I made the legs long ago for your mother…but too late. She had already fled my house for your father by the time they were ready."

In the waning light of evening, her golden eyes were soft. "I think you have learned what she learned. Not all perceived sanctuaries are what we think they are, but that doesn't mean we have to give up on life. We can always move on."

They were sweet words, but they couldn't do anything about the facts. I gestured to my tail, then out to the Mother Ocean that would never be mine again, and finally up to the Palace where I had no place either.

The Sea Witch smiled, just a little. "There are always more possibilities than you can think of in the midst of despair, granddaughter—more than you can imagine."

She slid back under the water, so that I was terrified that she had gone for good, but when she returned, clutched in her hand was another long see-through pod.

"I was not quick enough to let your mother seek out the world she wanted. She wanted to see the world beyond Mother Ocean, and I would not give it to her. Now you have that chance. You will become the most amazing creature, darling granddaughter, a creature that has lived in the sea, on the land, and finally in the air itself."

She ripped open the package and a pair of beautiful brass and silk wings unfurled themselves before me. I gasped, and the legs began to play a different tune; it was light and hopeful. After a moment of contemplation, I glanced at my syrienne grandmother, and mimed drinking a potion. I did not care to have that experience again.

She laughed, just a little. "No potion this time, granddaughter. You have already sacrificed your voice and your tail. These are yours without pain."

Suddenly Roan seemed petty, and my hopes those of a child learning to walk. Instead of a life as a cossetted princess of the ocean or the land, I would become something else entirely.

I slipped the wings on over my shoulder and spread them wide. Just like the legs, these wings knew what to do. What could I do with them and the sound of the music in my legs? Would I see distant lands and become a creature of myth?

"Go, find out," the Sea Witch said, a faint gleam in her golden eyes.

As I rose into the air, music surrounding me, I looked out over Mother Ocean. In the waves I could see the heads of my sisters bobbing in time to the waves. I raised my hand to them and smiled.

I'll come back, the music sang, but first I must see what is out there.

Then the wings began to beat to my desires, and I set my sights on the distant horizon. Now I was a creature of the air. I left the palace and the prince far below me, and did not think of it again.

Little Red Flying Hood

TEE MORRIS

ONE

At the turn of the century, mankind had taken to the skies. Naturally, Death followed.

The Great War, so it was being called nowadays, "would be over by Christmas" so the recruiters had told Her Majesty's finest. What with England's Imperial might and Jerry scrambling to keep up, this should have been a dawdle. The Empire's fine fighting men would be back in time to light the pudding, enjoy a Cracker, and sing "Ding Dong Merrily on High" at Midnight Mass. Yes, most assuredly everyone would be home by Christmas.

That was three Christmases ago.

Now as Scarlett Quinn had done the two previous Christmases before, and as she would probably do in the holidays to come, her hands gripped the stick of her Bristol Scout. The throttle opened as the Frenchman shouted *"Contact!"* just before throwing the propeller into a spin. Once the engine gurgled and spluttered to life, the antiquated biplane rolled its way to the end of the runway, the crewman who also doubled as the camp's chef shouting something to her. It was probably the menu for tonight. It was his way of wishing her a safe flight, and an even safer return.

Scarlett adjusted her goggles, checked the modest Maxim mounted to her left, and breathed in the mix of fresh morning air and petrol fumes belching from her plane. As she continued down her checklist—the integrity of the rigging, flap response, fuel, ammunition—she recalled the words of a general passed on to her when she was admitted into the Royal Air Corps. *"The airplane is useless for the purposes of war."*

It must have been very easy to make that proclamation from a desk somewhere in London a long way from the secret airstrip in Rang-du-Fliers on the northern coast of France. Hers was a small operation to keep King and country informed. To Scarlett this nameless, faceless general only served as their inspiration.

It was time to prove him wrong. Once again.

As always there was the rush of delight, the elation when her Scout took to the skies, but Death was here too. She had seen it during her training at Curragh Camp. Even with the advancements of science, airships and aeroflyers, and now talk of amazing rockets that could propel Man to the Moon and back, Scarlett was regarded as "blessed with the luck of the Irish" in how she survived flight school, especially in the wake of her fearless manoeuvres in the skies.

That was her secret. Death might have followed the Empire to the skies, but she had avoided Death as she was the superior pilot.

The Scout had been refitted with better navigation equipment, a modest heating unit for her seat, and the camera apparatus housed in the undercarriage. Soon she would be over enemy territory, her solitary plane daring the Kaiser to come out and make quick work of her—at least that would be their intent. Scarlett would disappoint them in the end. She was bound to her duty to the Empire, and it would be her reconnaissance that would fulfil this pledge of hers.

A light flickered on her panel, and the small, backlit map that scrolled slowly across the screen indicated she had crossed into the Western Front. Peering over the side of her plane, Scarlett watched the scarred and pitted French countryside slowly slip underneath her. Even from her height, the toll this Great War was taking on France was unmistakable. Miles of strange patterns turned the nation into a giant, muddled jigsaw puzzle. Once she believed it had been an endless field of green—maybe not the bright and vibrant Kerry Green that she trained over, but still a place full of life.

In between the zigzags and odd arcs carved into the earth, she could see trench extensions which dared to reach in the direction of the enemy. Scarlett banked the plane to one side when she reached one of these peculiar branches. Earth crumbled at its end, inching westward from the German side to where the Allies were waiting for their next command.

Her Scout finished its circle, and then sank into a dive. Once levelled out, Scarlett threw a switch on the camera and slowed her airspeed down, just enough for her to catch a bit more detail on whatever was burrowing through the earth from the German side. The camera light was showing green, and she knew there would be plenty of film for this pass remaining. Just another minute or two and she should have an image to share with the RAC back at the base.

Just over the sound of her engine came the *pop-pop-pop* of gunfire. She tightened the grip on her stick. Any evasive movements would blur the images, making this run utterly pointless.

Her eyes quickly dipped to her right to where the modest set of six bombs were housed. Two standard fragment bombs, guaranteed to ruin anyone's day. A pair of "Screaming Banshees" that, on impact, deafened anyone not caught in the initial blast. The final two she knew were exactly what this rather sticky situation called for.

She reached for one of the Firestorms, and waited for another few hundred yards before rolling her plane. With her plane inverted, while the Germans scrambled to draw a bead on her, Scarlett dropped the Firestorm. Then she flipped the plane back upright.

She craned her neck to look back and saw the blanket of fire spread throughout that branch of the trenches. Just ahead was the end of the extension, and everything was an agitation of soil, rock, and mud. The Kaiser appeared to have something like a Manchester Mole, something the Army Engineers had been developing for the past year but could not seem to perfect.

Then came more shots, only this time from above her.

She had hoped it were Ornithopter Corps which, rumour had it, Jerry was reactivating in the more remote sectors of the Front. Recent intelligence indicated this was in order to concentrate more advanced weaponry for larger scale targets like Paris on the European Front, and Auckland in the Pacific Theatre. Ornithopter Corps were easy to outmanoeuvre, but when she looked up, her breath caught in her throat.

Descending on her like hawks on the hunt were two LVG's, and between them in the lead was a design she did not recognize from any previous RAC reports. A *triple*-winged plane, bright blue and white flashes coming from the engine's grill, descended on her, its most visible feature being speed. The aircraft's escorts struggled to keep up. Scarlett couldn't see the markings of either escort or lead plane, but the gunfire proved more than enough indication. Her borrowed time had just run out.

At the turn of the century, mankind had taken to the skies. Naturally, Death followed. Today, Death's gunsights were on Scarlett Quinn.

She opened the throttle up just a fraction more. Any more speed and she could easily ruin the images she was capturing. Just a few more yards, and then it would be her flying death-trap against Germany's best engineered planes. If the pilots had truly earned their wings, it would be quite a morning for her.

The green light for the camera switched to yellow. She was running out of film.

Bullets from above zipped by her Scout while from below came both pistol and rifle fire. Scarlett threw her gaze for a moment to the right wing. There were a few holes in the canvas Tink would have to mend, once back at base.

The trench extension ended. She gave her run another five seconds. Then she flipped the camera off, and pulled back on the stick.

Her stomach slipped further down into her bowels as the Scout angrily trembled and shook with the sudden ascent. No, her plane did not care for some of her antics. In fact, if an old, antiquated biplane could possess etiquette, it would have probably said rather pointedly, *"Manners, Miss Quinn!"* Instead it reluctantly ascended into the sky. The three German planes compensated and started a climb of their own.

"That's right, boys," she said, casting another glance over her shoulder. "Come on and chase me."

An indicator suddenly flared to life, warning a stall was imminent. Time to dive. Scarlett pushed the stick forward and now the sky banked away from view. Now, the barren, scarred countryside stretched out before her. Behind her, the three planes were closing in, their rifle fire trying to pick her out of the freezing cold air.

Scarlett banked hard to the left, ending her quick dive and taking her Scout in a wide loop to come around on the three planes. With one of the LVGs now to her left, she opened fire. Sparks danced along the one plane before its fuselage flashed and exploded into flames. The remaining LVG and triple-winged monster tumbled out of sight.

Knowing very little of this experimental plane, Scarlett focused her attention on the LVG. They were both evenly matched for speed, but when it came to armament and manoeuvrability...well, a red wagon with a slingshot outclassed her Scout. It would be design versus skill until she knew what quality of pilots these men were. The LVG banked hard right, turning his plane in a wild corkscrew fashion. Scarlett attempted a few rounds, but the plane kept slipping out of her sights. She quickly looked to either side of her for the strange, new plane, but it was nowhere to be seen.

When she turned her attention back to the LVG, the quick plane was halfway through an arch that would line him up for a strafing run across her own fuselage.

Scarlett pulled back hard on the Scout's stick, opening the throttle to coax as much speed as she could. Provided Tink's latest modifications were sound, the Scout would hold together, even as it shot upward, inverted, and then swooped down after the apex. The LVG overshot its own loop, and slipped in front of Scarlett. Her Scout was close enough to read the pilot's name painted into the canvas, but she didn't get enough time to commit it to memory as she pulled hard to the left, her bullets ripping through the enemy plane's engine.

When the LVG exploded, Scarlett only had seconds.

Her plane corkscrewed around flying debris, chunks of canvas, wire, and wood. It was only seconds but the flight felt as if Scarlett were lost in some horrific nightmare suspended thousands of feet in the air. Finally righting her plane as more bullets flew by, Scarlett looked everywhere but couldn't see her last remaining opponent.

Then the three-winged monster reappeared, flying up from underneath her. Tipping to its right, it flew alongside her, and now Scarlett could see the details in the plane. It was painted black, only the white outline of the German Cross visible in its tail section. The plane was longer than her own. She should have heard the ugly snarl of horsepower, but the plane made no sound whatsoever. From where the engine would have been, Scarlett could see those odd flashes of blue and white.

How was this thing staying in the air?

She caught a glimpse of something in red written along the bottom of the plane before it pitched almost at a perfect angle to the right, away from Scarlett, quickly disappearing over the horizon and heading for home.

He could have easily shot me down, Scarlett thought. *He left me alive. Why?*

An alarm rose from her dashboard. Before she glanced at what it pertained to, she saw the smoke. One of these Huns had managed to draw a bead on her, but from the protestations from the engine, it would not be serious enough to take her to ground. It would mean facing the wrath of Tink which, as Scarlett considered the holes in the canvas, could be worse than ditching her Scout in No Man's Land.

Scarlett switched the seat heater off, conserving the old bucket's resources—threadbare as they were—to the engine. She also chucked the remaining bombs in her cockpit, just to lighten the payload. Her eyes then came to the emergency release of the Maxim, slapdash secured to the left side of her plane. It was her only defence, albeit not much if the enemy came from any direction other than the left.

"Pay the Piper," she muttered to herself as she took hold of the release switch. "Fly another day."

The Maxim tumbled from the left side of the plane, and instantly the Scout lifted a few feet higher. Now it came down to luck. If she could coax the engine enough to get within sight of Rang-du-Fliers, then she could glide her in to a landing.

But what kind of landing? That remained to be seen.

TWO

ow come along, Tink, you're not still upset with me?"

The young woman's ebony skin glistened in the sunshine. Considering how cold it was in this present French winter, it was astounding that she was sweating.

Then Scarlett bit her bottom lip. It had been close on two weeks since her last reconnaissance mission, and Tink was *still* working on the Scout.

"You should just be lucky that my daddy had me spending time in the garage with my brothers instead of playing house like all the other river kids in Lafayette." She dabbed at the sweat across her brow as she added, "I will tell you somethin' right here and now, Red, my brothers wouldn't know where to start in keeping this thing in the air. The stress you put this rigging through…"

"Well you know, these planes do go through a bit of wear and tear."

"You don't say."

Scarlett's eyes narrowed on her mechanic. "There's no need for such cheek, Tink."

"I'm from the South. You could not handle the cheek I keep in my back pocket."

"At least you're talking to me again," she said, smiling.

"I suppose I am, Red."

She shot her mechanic a wry grin. "Would you please stop calling me that? Bad enough I got this wild mane of red hair, I don't need to be reminded of how it makes me stand out."

Tink laughed. "Why do you think I do it? Only way I can get back at you for this," she said, motioning to the battered plane. "Don't worry about it. I'll get her up in the air before the end of tomorrow."

The Scout was terribly outdated, alarmingly outgunned, and hardly worth the time and parts put into keeping her in the air; but for all of both Tink's and Scarlett's complaints, this was their only plane. It had been their only plane as it was expendable. That was the one word Scarlett hated using when it came to the Scout, but that was a painful truth about her assignment at Rang-du-Fliers. No one else wanted the assignment so close to the front. Everyone knew the risk. It was, though, how Scarlett could best serve. The intelligence she could gather would save countless lives.

"Just tell me it was worth it," Tink insisted.

"We sent the film over to the War Office." Scarlett shrugged. "No reply. No new orders. Not sure what to do here."

"Well, you can't fly and get your mind off things as is your wont, so you can always do what I do. Grab a bottle of wine, find the highest point you can, and watch the sunset."

"What good will that do me?"

"It will give you some perspective."

"You think I'm in need of it?"

"We all need it from time to time. Perspective," and she shrugged before returning to work on the plane, "or just a really good bottle of wine."

Scarlett gave her faithful mechanic a soft chuckle, and then walked out of the hangar, into the cloud-covered day. It was quiet without the sounds of patrols above. That baffled her as she half-expected the skies to be filled with British, French, or German planes. It had been two weeks since her encounter with that incredible flying machine and yet there was nothing in the sky to even indicate that anything out of the ordinary had happened. Whatever this machination was, it could very well be the advantage Jerry needed to take control of the skies.

She had written it up in her report, along with a description of the Mole-like device. So why had no one from the War Office contacted her yet? Why had there been no new orders? *They must have a good reason to maintain radio silence,* she thought as she crossed the open field to the small shed just opposite of the house.

Scarlett dialled in the sequence to the combination lock and then slid the door open. She threw the switch opposite the wooden platform underfoot and descended into the ground a few feet, squinting at the harsh lights of the Communications bunker.

"Do you always have to keep it so bright down here, Adams?"

"Considering I am out of the sun and living like a troll under Westminster Bridge, yes, Lieutenant Quinn," Adams said, giving her a stiff smile. Even as fair as her own complexion was, Scarlett found Communications Specialist Alabaster Adams so pale that he was practically opaque. Add to the colour of his skin the high, rigid cheekbones and his thin, lanky frame, and it would be believed he were a carved ivory statue come to life. "Scientists believe that the human body needs a certain amount of light daily as it can affect mood, attention spans, erotic desires…"

"You can stop there." Scarlett glanced at the empty "In" box, then looked at the æthermessenger. "Still nothing?"

"As of ten minutes ago, and the ten minutes before that…" He checked his pocket watch and nodded. "Yes, and ten minutes before that…"

"Point taken."

"Although I must confess this is the most interaction we have shared since my assignment." Adams sniffed. "I think I preferred the occasional visitation schedule."

"You are not a prisoner here. You can go on, stretch your legs, enjoy some *actual* French sunshine."

"But that would mean…" He swallowed nervously. "…going outside."

Scarlett blinked. "And the problem with that is…?"

"Lieutenant Quinn, there is a reason I am exceptional at what I do. Apart from understanding the nuances of atmospheric changes and how they affect æthersignals, and staying abreast on all manners of technological advancements, I tend to work best when in a *safe* environment."

"Like this bomb shelter, for example?"

"Exactly. You see, there are risks involved when going…" The corners of his mouth twitched, and then he continued. "…outside. Unknown elements that could, at a moment's notice, steal from your operation the best asset it possesses."

Scarlett nodded. "I should warn Tink then. She may be in danger."

Adams raised a single finger at her, then paused. Perhaps he thought better of what he was going to say. "To answer your original question, no. No message from Command or anyone else. Will that be all, Lieutenant?"

"At least for the next ten minutes, yes. I'll see myself out."

Scarlett usually did see herself out. Still, it was an understood acknowledgement between them that the conversation was done, and she would leave him to it. Whatever that "it" was in the time being.

Returning to the outside world, Scarlett looked up once more to the silent skies. A thought itched at the back of her brain, or not so much a thought as a memory. She should have heard the sound of this three-winged plane, but there had been only the snarl of her Scout.

And the pilot let her go. After taking down two of his own.

The silence was suddenly broken by the sound of engines, but these were not plane engines. These rumblings belonged to machinations more terrestrial. A car carrying three men led a large truck down the country road ending at their airfield. A muscle twitched slightly in her jaw as she looked at the Scout's hangar, then back to the three uniformed men drawing closer. Even at this distance, she could see how neatly pressed their uniforms were.

Three years of secrecy, now all at risk because of these daft tossers.

The truck broke off to trundle towards the hangar while the officers continued to where she stood in front of the cottage.

When the car came to a stop, Scarlett took another look skyward. All was still and quiet. However, she was not at ease. Not after what she saw in the skies over the Front.

"Miss Scarlett Quinn?" one of the gentlemen sitting in the back seat asked. A major. The one next to him was a colonel.

"You can call me 'Lieutenant' as that was my rank last time I checked."

The colonel raised an eyebrow. "That some right cheek you have there, Quinn."

"Colonel, have you enjoyed the pleasure of a flight over Rang-du-Fliers?"

"I cannot say that I have."

"Well then, Colonel, please allow me to tell you what you would see. From the air, my hangar would have looked like a barn. Nothing overtly fancy. Just a large barn. Our communications bunker would have looked like a shed, and our barracks a farmer's humble cottage. We're hidden in plain sight, sir. The Kaiser has no idea we're operating out of this location for well on to three years now." She walked up to the car and opened their door, sweeping her free hand in the direction of the cottage. "Three years of cover you lot are jeopardizing as you did not have the wherewithal to disguise yourselves. Park in the garage, if you can manage such a simple feat. Should be enough room for you."

The driver looked back at his superiors. The Major shrugged, picked up a large folder propped up by his feet, and slid out of the car. "You heard the lieutenant. Park in the garage and stay with the car."

Scarlett watched the car rumble its way around the back of the cottage before turning back to the two officers. "I have worked very hard with what the RAC graciously parted with, and I've managed to keep my operations secret and my intelligence reliable, all while staying alive. Next time you come unannounced, you may as well invite a marching band to herald your arrival."

"Now see here, lieutenant—"

"If I may speak freely, Colonel Barnswallow, Quinn here does have a point. We should have shown more caution."

The colonel kept an icy stare on his counterpart as they entered the barracks. It did not have to work too hard to pretend to be a cottage, because that was essentially what it was. The house had a small parlour for receiving and entertaining guests, a kitchen in the back promising a fine lunch, and a single staircase leading upstairs to where she and her crew would tuck in for the night.

"Would you gentlemen care for a coffee?" Scarlett asked.

"I would prefer tea, if you have it," Barnswallow said, tucking his hat under the crook of his arm.

"Coffee, thank you," the Major replied.

Scarlett nodded before calling out, "René!"

"*Oui?*" a gruff voice replied from the kitchen.

"Be a dear, and fix a coffee and tea for our guests."

"Anything for you, *mademoiselle?*"

"No, I'm fine." Scarlett motioned to the couch as she took a chair opposite of them. "So, Colonel Barnswallow. And Major…?"

"Oh, sorry, Major Harold Hemsworth," he said, offering his hand.

Scarlett brazenly accepted the offer. "Quite a handshake you have there, Major."

Hemsworth chuckled. "Before the war, I was a country lad. Spent my formative years chopping wood, hunting, that sort of thing."

"How does a woodsman like yourself rise in the ranks of the military?"

"Turns out I have a penchant for tank warfare." He blushed slightly. A rather endearing quality considering the man's standing. "Bit of a surprise, even to me."

Barnswallow cleared his throat. "Would you care to skip the pleasantries, Major, or must I remind you there is a war going on at present?"

"Ah, yes," and Hemsworth opened up the file he had been carrying.

Scarlett immediately recognized photographs pulled from her film. *Finally,* she thought.

"We have been reviewing your reconnaissance footage," Hemsworth began, "and what you presented us was exceptional, as always."

"Thank you," Scarlett said.

"In fact, that is why we are here. We need to discuss with you in detail about what you've captured here."

Her brow furrowed. "You came all the way out to Rang-du-Fliers to review my footage? We could have easily done that over encrypted æthermissives."

"No, lieutenant," Barnswallow said. "What you captured on film goes well beyond normal operations. Your footage went on a rather jolly jaunt between RAC Command to the War Office, and then…elsewhere."

"Elsewhere?"

Barnswallow took in a deep breath. "2 Whitehall Court."

A chill crept under Scarlett's skin. "The Secret Service Bureau?"

"Hence why there was a delay in responding to you," Hemsworth said, flipping through the photos as he continued. "There was a bit of a debate between the Foreign Section and a Ministry office that, quite frankly, I've never heard of vying for jurisdiction over something like this. The Ministry of Peculiar Occurrences does indeed have an extensive background in investigating the unusual and bizarre, but Cumming was adamant that this was to be a Bureau matter."

"I don't understand. I got a shot of what looks like a Manchester Mole. *Two weeks ago.* That digger technology is in Jerry's hands. At the rate they were digging—"

"We've notified the War Office about the digger," Hemsworth stated. "They have already intercepted the Mole. Quite the capture."

Scarlett tipped her head to one side. "Then why are you lot here?"

Hemsworth slipped a photo out of the stack. "This is why."

The photograph appeared as a white canvas with three objects imprinted in the upper-right quadrant. Unlike the images she had taken of the trenches, no details of these three objects were visible save for the fact that the centre object was a plane with three wings, flanked by two other planes with a common, easily recognizable design.

"I…took this?" Scarlett managed to say.

"And you're still alive," Hemsworth said. "Well done."

THREE

René had left two coffees and a tea. He mentioned something about how Scarlett would eventually ask for a coffee, so he took that extra step forward. He also eluded to the risk of Scarlett allowing her drink to go cold. Something to that effect. Scarlett could not be sure. Her attention never left the photograph of the three planes, one of which no one knew anything concrete about.

"I'm the only pilot who has seen this plane, captured it on film, and made it back to base?"

"Yes," Barnswallow said, taking a sip of his tea. "We have attempted several reconnaissance missions to confirm the rather dubious intelligence on this new plane design, only to have it fail miserably."

"The Fokker Driedecker or Dr.1," Hemsworth said, tapping his finger against the silhouette of the triple-winged plane, "and that is all we know about the plane at present that is not based on conjecture or wild rumour. So, yes, we are here to find out what you know. Perhaps confirm or deny what Jerry has up in the air."

"Were there any distinct markings or features of the aircraft, apart from that stacked wing design?"

Scarlett dropped the photo back on the file in front of them and sat back in her chair. She tried to will herself to drink the cup of coffee, but she wanted something stronger. "The plane was black. There was the outline of the Iron Cross near the tail section, but nothing out of the ordinary."

"What about the plane itself?" Hemsworth asked. "How did it fly?"

"It was silent. Quite mad, but that's how it was," Scarlett said, lightly pulling at her bottom lip as she ran through her memory of the flight. "I remember seeing from the engine compartment flashes of blue and white. Was not quite sure what to make of that." She looked up, catching Barnswallow and Hemsworth exchanging a look. "You know something about this?"

"How's your avionics history, lieutenant?" Hemsworth asked.

"I do what I can to know planes of the past and present."

"Just before the turn of century, we had aeroflyers like the Avro Five-tens. But there was an experimental Five-ten-A, a rather clever idea from Nikola Tesla which introduced electric engines as the power source."

"The Five-Ten-A's were in action with private companies like White Star Line," Barnswallow said. "They were used to fend off airship pirates, and proved quite effective."

Hemsworth nodded. "Diesel technology supplanted steam, and the notion of an electric-diesel aeroflyer, while bandied about, never really took hold."

"But this was silent," Scarlett insisted. "It made no sound whatsoever."

Barnswallow took another sip of tea, then took in a long slow breath. His scowl, not directed to anyone in particular, deepened. "While we have a hold over the oceans, I would dare say it is Jerry who owns the skies. Their understanding of aviation engineering is not only commendable, it is inspiring."

Scarlett exchanged looks with the men, and then she saw the plane clearly in her head again. "This Fokker plane is electric. *Completely* electric?"

"Electric cars were all the rage at the turn of the century," Hemsworth said. "A decade ago, they were averaging a hundred miles on a full cell. When you think of how far and how fast air travel has developed, it is not a stretch to think of how far battery technology has progressed as well."

"Jerry must have also cracked the problem with cold temperatures and the toll it takes on a battery's charge," Barnswallow added.

"Is there anything else you noticed about this plane?"

"I think I've told you everything," Scarlett said, but then she paused. "No, wait, there was something else painted on the plane. It was in German so I'm not sure exactly what it says."

"Stationed this close to the Front and you don't know the language?" Barnswallow huffed.

"Considering I am usually in the air, no, I thought it more necessary to know French in order to blend in." Scarlett pinched the bridge of her nose, closed her eyes, and tried to recall what she had caught a glimpse of. "Grover Bosser Wolf, I think. I do remember 'Wolf' being the only word I remotely recognized."

"Was it Großer Böser Wolf?" Hemsworth asked.

"Yes, that was it. Grobber…Grubber…eh, what you said."

Hemsworth, tapping his fingers together, glanced over to Barnswallow, then looked back to Scarlett. "Something we were afraid of."

"You know who this fellow is, don't you?"

Barnswallow fidgeted in the corner of his couch while Hemsworth finished his coffee, and then appeared to gather up his courage. "Maximiliane Adolphina Vogelberg von Wolff. She's also known as the Big Bad Wolf."

"The Aces of Aces," Scarlett whispered. "She…let me go. She could have added me to her kills and she let me go. Why?"

"Again, this is why there was such a debate as to whom would take jurisdiction over this case."

"As much as I loathe to repeat myself," grumbled Barnswallow, "Cumming was adamant. About many things."

"What do you mean by that?" Scarlett asked.

The door flying open could not have been timed better, even if it were on stage with the best skilled actors. *"Red, you won't believe what we got in the hangar!"*

"Red?" chuckled Hemsworth.

Just. Lovely. As if the nickname wasn't bad enough, Tink had to use it in mixed company. "Gentlemen, this is my mechanic, Tina Keller."

"American?" barked Barnswallow. "And here I thought the Yanks wanted nothing to do with our merry little war."

"Tink is originally from the United States, Colonel, but she emigrated here a few years ago. She's managed to keep the Scout flying for the past two years."

"So no, I'm not here representing a country that doesn't want me, sir," Tink said, her gaze brazenly fixed with Barnswallow's. "I'm representing a country that were a bit more welcoming. The place I now call home."

"I see you set a shining example to your support staff," Barnswallow noted.

"Wait a moment," Hemsworth said. He was visibly distracted. "You're flying a Scout? A Bristol Scout?"

"Only plane they'd give us dainty little ladies," and then Tink's scowl turned into an incredibly bright smile, "until today!"

Now it was Scarlett who found herself off-kilter. "I—what?"

"Lieutenant, the Foreign Office and the RAC are working together on this mission," Hemsworth began, pulling out a dossier from underneath the pile of photographs in front of him. "We need you back in the sky and over enemy territory. We have a mission for you. We're ready to equip you with whatever you need."

"Reconnaissance?"

"Not this time." He presented her with the sealed orders. "All the details are there, but we need you to make contact with an agent deep undercover in Halle. You are to meet with this operative who will give you the schematics to this experimental fighter plane."

Scarlett looked at Tink. She could only assume her shock was just as visible as her mechanic's. "Gentlemen, you have me at a loss. This is not what I do. I do *aerial* reconnaissance. You're asking me to engage in ground operations across enemy lines? Don't you have spies that are better trained for this sort of thing?"

"Lieutenant," Barnswallow said, "this is where we need your particular skills as a pilot. We're asking you to fly into enemy territory and fly out without detection."

"And if you are detected," Hemsworth said, "we need a pilot skilled enough to either evade or take down the Big Bad Wolf."

"*Take down* the Big Bad Wolf?" Scarlett's laugh was harsh, grating. "I didn't outfly her. She let me go."

"Perhaps Captain Wolff saw something in you. Perhaps she recognized a raw talent in your skills. She could have shown a moment's compassion as your Scout was hardly worth..." His voice trailed off. Apparently, he heard himself clearly.

"You're suggesting the Big Bad Wolf took pity on me?"

Hemsworth went to answer, but he appeared to be searching for what to say. He looked to Barnswallow who simply shrugged in silent reply. "Well," Hemsworth stammered, "I wouldn't have put it that way..."

"Lieutenant, perhaps you could come with us to your hangar," Barnswallow said, placing his cap back on his head. "We are offering you an opportunity that I believe will be to your liking."

Scarlett had so many questions on her tongue, she could taste them. They all tasted bitter, and the longer they lingered on her tongue, the angrier she grew. They were going to bribe her with, from the looks of Tink bouncing on the balls of her feet, an upgrade of some kind to the Scout.

"Fine, I will hear you out," Scarlett huffed as she rose to her feet, "so long as you feel this little trip south of Calais wasn't a colossal waste of time."

"I can't wait for you to see this," Tink squealed with delight.

Then she sprinted ahead of the three of them. Scarlett and the two officers took long strides to the hangar but were not necessarily making a mad dash of it.

"So you have an operative in enemy territory?" Scarlett asked. This was not an acknowledgement nor was it an agreement. *I am just curious,* she told herself. "Why has no one else made contact? Why hasn't anyone from the Bureau bothered to get these plans out before now?"

"Lieutenant, the amount of bad information we receive from field reports is alarming," Hemsworth said. "We are tired of chasing leads and believing intelligence that only cost lives in the end."

"You mean, like the Gallipoli Campaign?" Scarlett asked.

She heard the footsteps behind her abruptly stop. She turned to face both officers, Barnswallow's face beet root red as he looked upon her.

"This is why you are being so careful, are you?" Scarlett pressed before resuming their walk to the barn. "I am a backwater, remote operation.

Resources so threadbare they are a right joke. I have a team that is the best at what they do, and they make certain our intelligence is consistently trustworthy. This mission you want me to undertake, is one of those missions like Gallipoli. You are less than optimistic about the outcome, but you want to make certain whomever you send in knows what they are signing up for."

"You lost friends at Gallipoli?" Hemsworth asked.

"Very perceptive, Major."

"As are you, Lieutenant. You are exactly right. We did not want to risk another operation based purely on intelligence we could not confirm. Then, two weeks ago—as luck would have it—you did."

"We will lose this war if we do not take control of the skies," Barnswallow said, his colour a bit closer to normal but his dander still up. "This Fokker could tip the scales in favour of Jerry, and we cannot have that."

"And we intend," Hemsworth said, pointing into the hangar, "to make sure you have what you need to face the Big Bad Wolf without fear."

The sight of the plane nearly made her faint. It looked as if it were a Sopwith Camel, but with slight differences in the design. The wings, instead of reaching straight out, were angled back by ten degrees or so. Underneath the fuselage, there was mounted a fat cylinder that appeared to be directly connected to the plane's powerful engine. The twin machine guns mounted on the fuselage were thrilling to see, but also equally thrilling were the small turrets mounted on either side of the tail section.

"Lieutenant Quinn," Barnswallow said, "this is the Sopwith Hornet, a prototype of our own. The engine is based on the electric motor with range extender that the Avro Five-Ten-As utilized in their service."

"The armament is similar to the Camel in that you have two synchronized Vickers in a fixed, forward-firing position," Hemsworth offered, "but you also have the two defensive measures on the tail of the Hornet."

"Defensive measures?" Scarlett asked.

"It looks like a smoke screen of some description," Tink called from the plane. Of course she was already going over the beastie, looking to see where she could make her own improvements. "The other canon, I've not quite figured out what they fire."

"Flares," Hemsworth said. "They are intended to distract or even blind your opponents. One time use only, though."

Scarlett shook her head. "With all these additions and that"—her head cut back and forth along the wing— "whatever this is, will it get in the air?"

"I assure you, Lieutenant," Hemsworth said, his smile wide and proud, "this will not only stay in the air but it will make quick work of anything that tries to take you out of the air."

Scarlett turned around to face the two officers. "Including the Big Bad Wolf?"

"That is the problem we are facing at present," Barnswallow said. "We have hard intelligence and your testimony corroborating it. In the Hornet, you have a fighting chance against the Big Bad Wolf, but the Fokker prototype we are led to believe is the superior aircraft. It's going to be your skills against hers."

"Get into Germany, meet your operative, come back with the plans of this Fokker aircraft. Just like that?"

"Just like that," Hemsworth said. "We can give you a few days to get used to her before taking her behind enemy lines."

"No time like the present, Red!" Tink called. "Let's fire her up!"

Scarlett could feel someone standing next to her. It was Hemsworth, and she suddenly realized how tall the major was. He looked down at her with a mischievous grin plastered across his face.

"This nickname of yours," he said, looking down at her, "it suits you."

"Does it now?"

"Quite," and then he winked. Scarlett did not care for how her knees suddenly felt uncertain. "Little Red."

Height jokes? This mission was getting better and better by the second.

ENTR'ACTE

This was not the Halle she grew up in. This was not the Germany she knew. She did not want to die in such a place so sad, so barren. Outside her cottage windows, Elsa once saw the Hallerbos standing along her village borders, tall and imposing as old, wizened guardians assuring her hamlet they were all safe from harm.

Now whenever she looked out her windows, all that remained was a barren field, save for the factory where she worked. A giant structure housing machines of destruction, and a long strip of packed earth that served as an airfield.

No, this was not Elsa's Halle. Had not been so for a long, long time.

Perhaps that was why, in the dim lighting of this inn, no one took notice of her sitting alone. She was a crone enjoying her porridge, the mug of beer beside her perhaps warming her old bones against the winter's chill. She was invisible, and that was a very good thing to be in this world. This new Germany that would stand against the oppression of self-appointed masters. *"England tightens the belt of humiliation around our loins, condemning us to the abyss! We have marched blindly towards calamity for too long. Hold out and triumph!"* as the posters told her throughout the town.

Tonight, however, she had to be invisible. She would need it to survive in this new world.

"Gutentag," the young man said, a small tray in his hands with a meal identical to her own on it. His German was polished, perfect. "Might I sit with you? I would love to chat with someone while I eat."

Es beginnt also, she thought.

"I am afraid I am not one for idle talk," she replied, as she was instructed to.

"Then, perhaps we can talk politics?" he returned politely.

She nodded. As he sat down, Elsa whispered to him in English, "You should be careful whom you speak with in Halle."

The spy blinked. "You speak English?"

"I've not always been an old country woman. I was fortunate to have lived a very comfortable life. I travelled when I could. The wonders of science made the world an easier place to see." She patted him on his hand. "Your German is flawless. Not a hint of the local accent. That will be your undoing, I fear."

He took a sip of his beer. "Any advice then?"

"Keep your conversations short. One or two word sentences." She bobbed her head back and forth, then added, "If you have to engage in conversation, slur some of your words together, as if you have drunk too much. And speak slower."

"You know, if you are looking to leave Germany, I have no doubt your knowledge would be most welcome back at the London offices."

She cast a wary glance around her. Conversations continued, beers were shared, and still her invisibility held. "You make it sound as if I have a choice. I have lived for so long in this country and you think I could leave it so easily? Without a thought? Why? Because this is not a Germany I no longer believe in? Considering my age, it would not be such a great loss if I were to pack what few things I own that I treasure, take what savings I still have, and purchase a train ticket. Go somewhere close to *Teutoburger Wald.*"

"A forest? You want to see a forest?"

"Not a forest. Teutoburger Wald. This is a forest that holds history, possesses such beauty as would make you weep. I could go there, accept the eternal embrace of the forest, lose myself within the wood, and gently fade into nothingness."

Such a death, Elsa knew, was not noble, nor graceful, nor elegant. It was surrender. Weak. Cowardly. To wander into a forest and die like a stray dog, alone. This new, bold Germany threatened to take everything away from her, starting with the trees.

"Forgive me for being presumptuous, Miss Katzer, but you always have options. I dare say you know that better than anyone."

Her eyes narrowed on the young man now tucking into his stew. The English were being promoted as many things, but "shrewd" was not one of the words the government had used.

From the looks on his face, he was impressed with the beef stew served here. The man needed to see more of the world. "Did you get the plans?"

"I did," she said. "Safe at home."

"Very good, Miss Katzer. Are you certain I cannot entice you to take advantage of our offer for safe passage?"

"*Nein,*" she replied without a moment's hesitation. "I will not leave my home."

The man's brow furrowed. "But you just said you no longer believe in Germany."

"*This* Germany," she clarified pointedly. "I do not believe in those who rule over it at present. Particularly, those who believe a weapon such as this would return things to normal, to the way things were before this supposed Great War began. This *Schwarzer Geist* is the kind of weapon that would not be content with a victory over the Allies."

"Schwarzer Geist?" the Englishman asked. "The Black Ghost?"

Elsa nodded. "With the sweetness of victory upon their lips, would you believe our leaders capable of merely dismantling their Black Ghost and allowing peace to rule?" She laughed bitterly before taking a drink. "These men and women would make Europe bleed by pushing their boundaries further. Perhaps even rule, for a change, over your precious United Kingdom."

The spy raised an eyebrow. "The Kaiser can certainly try, but I think he will find our lion quite difficult to tame."

Her eyes narrowed on him. "It is arrogance like that which brings countries to war."

For a few moments, they remained silent as they ate. Elsa was not particularly hungry, but that was what this was all about, wasn't it? Deception. Espionage. Treason.

Finally, the Englishman spoke. "Your contact will meet you tomorrow afternoon. 2:00 p.m. If she doesn't show by 2:05 p.m. I suggest you buy a ticket for that forest you so desperately want to see."

"How will I know her?"

"She'll call you 'Grandmother' as she's traveling under the guise of your granddaughter."

Elsa paused. "That is my code name?"

"Yes."

"Delightful," she huffed. "And my reply?"

"Whatever you like, so long as you call her 'Little Red' somewhere in there."

Elsa polished off her beer and began to bundle herself up. "Then I shall see your contact at 2 p.m." She stood but then leaned over the table to whisper to him. "If I'm not home for any reason, tell your contact to help herself to a blanket. It can get chilly in Halle."

"Thank you, Miss Katzer..."

Her whisper turned harsh, pointed. "Listen to me, boy—tell Little Red to help herself to a blanket. It can get very, very cold. Tell her that. Word for word."

His brow knotted as he stammered, "I will."

With a curt nod, she said, "Good night then."

"You have no idea the difference you are making."

"I will believe it when this Great War is done," and she eased away from the table, her body suddenly in need of her bed and a good night's sleep.

Perhaps Elsa should not have been so brusque with the young man. He was only trying to reassure her she was doing the right thing, but the spy's gesture only reminded her of the war machine her country had become. The men in their sharp uniforms had come to her door, complete strangers believing themselves to be close acquaintances with Elsa. *We are Germany, and we must do our part for the Empire,* they had told her cheerily. Her part—small as it was—in keeping the brave men and women safe on the Western Front involved manning a trolley of simple nibbles and drinks for the factory. This would be her part in the greater war machine. She was a modest cog turning the gears that kept larger parts moving. The others—engineers, designers, and line operators—would provide the newest and most innovative weapons for the troops, for the greater glory of their country, a country no longer answering to the English.

"The difference you will make will not be seen," the nice young man in the sharp dress uniform told her, *"but it will be appreciated."*

This menial task at the factory was nothing significant, but it did brighten the mornings and afternoons of those who worked there. To some, she was invisible. Hardly a bother to her as it meant more distance between her and this brave, new Germany. This would be the Germany where she would die, like it or not. It was not the surrender she had once contemplated, but merely a gentle resignation. At least the Germany she knew and loved would remain in her heart.

Then Elsa discovered some advantages about her invisibility at the factory. She could access places deemed *"Verboten"* to others. No matter the job or the duty, or the security clearance, people needed their tea and biscuits, or perhaps a cup of coffee to pick up their spirits and keep them alert. This included the men and women that dreamt up such astounding creations as that new plane. The *Schwarzer Geist*. Silent as the grave, black as pitch. This was the sort of modern marvel, the sort of weapon, that could end the war but to what purpose and what end?

On watching its maiden flight, watching it soar like a dark eagle over Halle, Elsa knew the Germany she loved so dearly was done. In its place would be this war machine, committed on having the world on bended knee, subservient.

She remembered that night at the inn, openly weeping at her table as she ate her porridge. It was unusual for her to eat at the local inn, but she wanted to be around people that night. She didn't want to feel so alone.

That was when Johann, the local baker and a friend, took a seat across from her, took her hand, and asked what troubled her so. She told him and he listened. He nodded. His hand squeezed hers gently. When Elsa was done, she waited for her friend to reply, possibly with propaganda-inspired words of comfort.

What Johann proposed to Elsa stopped her tears. All it would take would be one action on her part. One action that could change everything.

When an evening shift presented itself, Elsa was to do her part for Germany. Attend on those working late into the night. Nothing out of the ordinary. As was her way, she pushed her tea and coffee trolley along the hallways, offering a cheery smile and a cup of warmth against the cold weather. The guards were still omnipresent, but perhaps less attentive. She was, after all, the kindly old lady that served tea, coffee, and delightful pastries that cured hunger pangs arriving in the early morning hours. Elsa was, at least, that "kindly old lady" to those who noticed. Her invisibility would be more than just the distance she preferred, but on this particular night it would be her advantage.

Her trolley trundled past security guards engrossed in their own conversations. Some of the smaller offices were occupied, but only one of the scientists looked up from their work only to return to it with no interest of a late night treat. Eventually, she reached the main workroom of this floor. Before her stretched long tables that she recognized under the light of day, usually occupied by engineers and designers working on their latest creations, always looking for ways to improve what rumbled across the earth, sliced through the ocean, or soared high in the air.

Elsa pushed her cart to the back of the office, back to where the filing cabinets stood. When she stopped at the long, wide blueprint cabinet, Elsa held her breath. She could hear a soft thumping in her ears. Her heartbeat was running faster than rabbits in the meadow. Apart from that she was alone.

Her eyes ran across the small plates until she found the drawer dedicated for aviation. Gingerly, Elsa pulled the drawer open. Her hands then fumbled in her apron pocket for the small torch she had brought with her. She twisted the small cylinder that flared to life in her hands. Again, she held her breath as her gaze went back to the hallways outside.

Still nothing. Not a sound. All alone.

The fingers of her free hand continued to flip back blueprint after blueprint until finally she saw the precise renderings of the triple-winged plane. Slipping it out of the pile, the plan fluttered lightly in the air before settling on the wide desk before her. Elsa looked up again to the door as she snuffed the electric light out of her hand. Confident she was alone, Elsa gingerly folded the plan once, then again, and one final time, assuring it would be a size that would fit inconspicuously in a tray reserved for small scones. Normally, this tray would be connected to a warming element of some description, but on this particular night she had disconnected any wires leading to it. This bottom drawer, and the one above it, were cold. She wanted to make certain that the plan was in no danger of being damaged.

She could still remember the sky's hue that early morning as she bid the guards at the main gate a pleasant farewell. It was a dappling of purple and blue against the heavy darkness, now receding as the sun slowly rose. A new day, in so many ways. As Johann instructed her, she was now to return to the inn and wait to meet the baker's friend. The spy. She was now part of the underground network working against the German Empire.

"Are you certain I cannot entice you to take advantage of our offer for safe passage?"

The gesture from her English contact was tempting, in case of capture; but why risk everything only to run from the place she called home? It would be as ridiculous as starting a garden in April only to tend to it in September. No, if she were caught, she would die in her country, content in her actions. In doing what was right.

Elsa walked into the warmth of her humble cottage, the cold now making her more than ready for that good night's rest. The *tick-tock-tick-tock* of her cuckoo clock was drowned out by the call of the clock's bird. It was far later than she preferred it to be, but she desperately needed something to warm up her old bones. Perhaps back at the inn she should have ordered the stew. It did look rather hearty.

"Guten Abend, alte Frau," came the silky female voice from behind her.

Elsa's hand lightly slapped against her chest as she spun around to the darkened corner of the cottage.

The long match hissed and flared to life, and then the bright flame reached into the lantern which cast a warm glow around the stranger in her home. She then took the match, its wood now curling on itself as the flame grew, and lit the thin cigar trapped between her lips. Two drags later, the sweet smell of the tobacco lifted into the air around them both.

"Been aching to enjoy this," the stranger said, contemplating the small cigar between her fingers. "Having it lit when you walked in though would possibly have alarmed you terribly."

The woman, from the looks of her uniform, was an officer, but that was all Elsa could tell at the moment. Her long black boots were polished to a flawless sheen while the silver buttons in her waistcoat and cloak twinkled in the light of her lantern. The woman's eyes were as black as her hair, pulled back into a tight bun. Elsa's gaze followed the cigar from the intruder's ruby red lips to the small saucer she recognized from her own cupboard. Right next to the small plate lay a pistol, its handle turned towards the stranger.

"Where are my manners?" the mysterious woman asked as she removed her cap and placed it across her lap. "Hauptmann Maximiliane Adolphina Vogelberg von Wolff."

"Elsa Katzer."

"Yes, I know. The tea trolley lady." Her smile did little to put Elsa at ease. "I know a great deal about you."

Elsa remained stock still. She would not make it to the door before this captain would gun her down. "Did you come into my home to ask for something in particular? I have not started baking yet for tomorrow."

"Oh that is very kind of you, but no, I am quite content with those chocolate chip scones of yours. They are delicious." Maximiliane took up her tiny cigar, and said, "I will miss them."

Und so endet es, Elsa thought to herself.

"We have some unpleasantness before us, you know this," the captain stated quite plainly, "but we can make this less tiresome, less inconvenient, if you tell me where the plans to the Black Ghost are."

Elsa kept her gaze with the woman. Perhaps this was not the end, after all.

Still, she would have liked to see Teutoburger Wald just one more time.

FOUR

This was Scarlett's fourth day with the Hornet, and she honestly thought that she would drop the somewhat silly euphoria she enjoyed whenever she flew it. No such luck. She had remained loyal to her faithful, if not somewhat well-worn, Brighton Scout; but that flying death-trap was a distant memory now. With additional modifications from Tink and Major Hemsworth offering what seemed to be limitless resources, the Hornet was ready for a flight into enemy territory.

Getting into Germany she knew would not be a problem. It was getting out that concerned her the most.

Just stay on the mission directives, she could hear Hemsworth reassuring her again and again. *Stick to that path and you will be back in France safe and sound with the plans to this Fokker prototype. Easy as pudding.*

Hemsworth was not the one flying into enemy territory. Although, he did assure her support. What that entailed, she could not be certain.

The Hornet stayed low on the horizon, the agreed upon colour making her difficult to spot by any patrol in the air which, according to this experimental proximity warning system Hemsworth had installed, was of no concern now. The skies were clear, and the flight plan that she, Tink, and Hemsworth had plotted would take her to a small field just outside of

Halle. From there, she would need to obtain transportation of some sort, then rendezvous with "Grandmother" at her house.

A yellow light flickered on her panel. The map scrolling across her dashboard indicated the landing coordinates just ahead. Scarlett took the Hornet even lower, eased up on the throttle, and hoped the ground underneath would be firm enough to handle a landing. Lower and lower still, until finally she felt the Hornet touch ground. The plane hopped up in the air and then touched down a second time.

She really needed work on her landing in this plane.

Once the Hornet powered down, Scarlett draped the netting over it. From the air, it would look nothing more than a patch of heavy grass. To passers-by it would look like something covered up under netting, so hopefully, this rendezvous would be a quick affair. The sooner she would be back up in the air, the happier she would be. Scarlett still found this mission to be a bit of a fool's errand, but she was duty bound and had her orders.

The Hornet, she begrudgingly admitted, did take the sting out of the madcap nature of the mission. She just hoped she would return to the airbase and have the time to truly enjoy all the wonderful machinations her new plane had to offer.

Scarlett pulled out of her jacket a small metal box no bigger than her hand. Pressing the latch, the lid flipped up and revealed the two larger lenses housed within it. She took in a quick scan of the countryside for anything worthy of concern. It was rather quiet in this part of the German Empire, something that she found both delightful and unsettling. The Germans were occupying the nearby city of Brussels, but from what she could see there was very little going on in this low-lying country. She had certainly expected more foot patrols.

Snapping the binoculars shut, Scarlett flipped open the cover of her wristwatch. The window of her rendezvous was closing quickly. She needed to get to Halle and get there fast.

Stepping carefully into the open, Scarlett headed east, into the direction Hemsworth's maps indicated would be Grandmother's house. Around her, pastures stretched for miles, but there was a farmhouse a few hundred yards ahead of her. Perhaps if she found a bicycle that would get her to Grandmother's house with a few minutes to spare.

Scarlett checked the perimeter of the barn. So far, no one about to cock up her plans. She pushed one of the main doors aside and slipped in.

It was a barn, reminiscent of the ones back home in Ireland. There was also a modest work bench with a variety of tools both scattered across the table and hanging on a pegboard above it. Scarlett then saw her chariot—an old Hildebrand & Wolfmüller.

"Well now, aren't you a sight?" For a motorcycle nearly twenty years old, this farmer kept it quite pristine. "I hope you run as good as you look."

Guiding the cycle outdoors, Scarlett gave a quick look around the barn. Once she started up this metal monster, the peaceful tranquillity of this countryside would be a memory. Satisfied she was alone, Scarlett risked it and coaxed the motorcycle to life.

The bike snarled and growled as it zipped her across the green fields of the German Empire. She checked her watch again. It looked as if she would reach Grandmother's House in plenty of time. Back into the air and over to France quick as she pleased? That suited her just fine. Yes. That would be splendid.

After a few minutes of dipping up and down hills, Scarlett found herself on a small dirt road, heading east to the small city of Halle. The rendezvous, according to intelligence, was somewhere outside the city, closer to where a forest once stood. Scarlett opened up the throttle and made quick work of the road. She paused at a sign indicating Halle was just ahead of her. Scarlett flipped open her map folio, checked her bearings once again, and then headed off.

Just stay on the mission directives. Stick to that path and you will be back in France safe and sound.

Mission Directives: Get into Germany, get the plans from Grandmother, and then get out. No heroics. No sabotage. Just get the plans and then get the hell out of here. It sounded simple. Almost too simple.

Stop trying to muck it up, Scarlett chided herself. *You can do this.*

Following a hill downward, Scarlett's gaze passed over a barren patch of earth where she could tell a forest of some description once stood. Now she could see in its place a factory with two hangars, a test track for automobiles, and a large runway. *The Kaiser stays busy here,* she thought to herself. There were also small clusters of homes visible, and Scarlett soon picked out the cottage described to her by Allied operatives.

According to Bureau's contacts, Grandmother's house was a typical brown colour, but distinguished by bright blue shutters and a vegetable garden to the right of it. *Sign out front should read Katzer,* Hemsworth had told her. *In the verification greeting, make sure to refer to her as Grandmother. And remember to listen for your code name as well. It's Little Red.*

Hemsworth thought it was cute. Scarlett wanted to clock him with a spanner.

She pulled up outside the gate of the humble cottage and checked her watch. She was early. Hopefully that wouldn't be a problem.

Her knuckle rapped on the door three times. No answer.

One more thing, Red, and our contact was pretty adamant about this, she suddenly recalled. *If Grandmother is not home for any reason, you should to help yourself to a blanket. It can get chilly in Halle.*

Really? That was what she was to do if her contact was nowhere to be found? Bundle up and wait? It was too easy to think this was her own personal Gallipoli unfurling in front of her.

She knocked on the door again. There was a pause before she heard a voice call out with some effort, "Come in, child. Do come in."

The door opened with a prolonged squeak, unsettling Scarlett all the more. The curtains were drawn, and what light was present did little to illuminate the house. There was a soft *tick-tock-tick-tock* of a beautiful cuckoo clock. It was a shame Scarlett had not been closer to two o'clock as she would have loved to hear it go off. There were the remains of a fire in the hearth, with a small wisp of smoke disappearing into the chimney.

From upstairs Scarlett heard coughing.

"Up here, dear," came a weak voice. Grandmother was not sounding so good.

"Coming on up, Grandmother," Scarlett said as she climbed the steps up to the bedroom.

The light up here was not much better, but it was considerably warmer. The air was still, and from the half-shadows created by a single lantern, Scarlett could see a form moving in the dark. Another hacking cough came from the woman under the covers.

This was the operative the Allies were counting on? This mission was growing more and more ridiculous by the minute.

"Are you sick, Grandmother?" Scarlett asked.

"Frightfully sick, child," her contact croaked. "Come closer so I can see you better."

Scarlett's eyes were beginning to adjust to the dimness of the bedroom. Grandmother's skin was quite pale, but the eyes staring back at her were quite dark. In fact, they appeared black. Like a doll's eyes.

"Grandmother, what big eyes you have," Scarlett said.

"The better to see you with, my dear," Grandmother replied.

Scarlett took a step forward. Grandmother's hands were not visible. They were clutching something underneath the blankets. "Grandmother, what big hands you have."

"The better to hug you with, my sweet child."

She braved another step forward and she could see Grandmother's smile. "Grandmother, what big teeth you have."

"The better to—"

Scarlett's fist shot out quick as a lightning strike, catching both the top visible teeth as well as the soft spot just underneath Grandmother's nose. The woman's head rocked back, giving Scarlett the chance to grab at the woman's gown and pull her into two more punches. The pistol, a Luger P08, fell out from underneath the covers.

"I just gave you the verification greeting three times, lady," and Scarlett knocked the woman back into the shadows with a Glasgow Kiss. "You are no grandmother of mine."

Scarlett pulled the unconscious woman out of the bed and turned up the lamp's flame to see this hostile stranger up close. From the looks of the uniform, she appeared to be an officer. High rank, maybe a captain. The uniform also looked as if it had been slept in so whatever happened to her contact must have happened the other night, and this woman had been waiting for her. Scarlett immediately went to the window. No sign of reinforcements. She could guess as to why there were no guards. Perhaps they were given orders to wait until a check-in was missed, and then what? They were to storm the house?

The cuckoo clock made her jump with a start. This was the time she was supposed to arrive. This had to be her final check-in. If not, they will probably give her five minutes before an extraction.

If Grandmother is not home for any reason, tell your contact to help herself to a blanket. It can get chilly in Halle.

Not *"Wait for me"* or *"Make yourself at home"* but specifically to get a blanket.

Scarlett's eyes darted to every corner of the cottage until finally coming to fall on a closet. She wrenched open the door, and let out a scream as an old woman's body toppled out. This must had been "Grandmother" and from the looks of her face and the condition of her bent, broken fingers, that bitch unconscious in the bedroom must have tried to torture her for the whereabouts of the Fokker schematics. Instead, she had been beaten to death.

"I'm so sorry," Scarlett whispered.

Her gaze then jumped to the wardrobe open in front of her. She reached up to the heavy blankets folded neatly on the higher shelf and shook the top blanket. When she unfurled the second blanket, the blueprint slipped free.

Scarlett bent back an open corner of the schematic and read the word "Fokker" and also saw written underneath the numerical designation the words *Schwarzer Geist.* She knew very little German, but recognized the second word there. Ghost. This was it.

With a final look to the old woman, Scarlett ran for the door and nearly tore it off its hinges. She stuffed the blueprint into one of the bike's saddlebags and then started up the engine. She cast a quick glance around her, and then she saw the truck slowly working its way towards the cottage. Scarlett mounted the bike and headed back up the hill, back the way she came. With any luck, she would have a five-minute head start on Jerry. If she could keep up the speed, perhaps she could make this lead a ten-minute head start.

One…two…three…four… Scarlett was trying desperately not to count the seconds or even preoccupy herself with whatever time was slipping away. She was also trying not to continuously look over her shoulder. She had to keep driving forward, keep pushing the cycle as hard as she could. What good would it do if she saw over her shoulder this strange woman that she punched several times, accompanied by a truck full of German soldiers? There would be nothing for her to do but try and hold her lead.

Still, she threw a quick glance behind her. No one else was there.

"Stay on the path, Scarlett," she whispered out loud, "just stay on the path and you'll be home before you know it."

The countryside did not seem to pass her as quickly as it did when she first arrived, but just up ahead were the familiar hills that she had ridden over. She could still see the faint impression left by her bike wheel on the trip in.

"I will not look behind me," she insisted. "I will not look behind me…"

On cresting another hill, just within sight, Scarlett could see her camouflaged Hornet. If her head start was indeed that ten minutes she speculated, she would need all of it to prep, taxi, and finally get up in the air.

Seventeen…eighteen…nineteen…twenty….

FIVE

uel was steady. Nothing to worry about there.

The electric engine, good for only thirty miles, she had kept offline. She had put the plane into a "Patrol" mode in order to utilize the petrol engine's ability to charge the battery while still in flight.

Proximity Alarm. The odd device that Tink was told not to take apart until Scarlett got back to base was reading all clear.

It should be a straight shot home from here.

Scarlett had been in the air for nearly an hour. The skies were clear, and below her the outskirts of the German empire were slowly creeping by. The Western Front would be underneath her within minutes which could mean unwelcome company in the air. All she needed to do was make it over the border, then maybe she could start breathing again.

The Proximity Alarm suddenly came to life, screeching madly while a yellow light pulsed. At least it wasn't the red light. Scarlett could only assume the red light meant things had gone completely pear-shaped. Yellow probably meant things were only inconvenient, but warranted attention.

Her eyes scanned the skies, but there was nothing above her. Underneath, however, she could see the outer edge of a patrol. Scarlett pulled back on the throttle and banked her Hornet a few degrees for a better look. Five LVG's, the Cross of the German Empire notably visible on the edges of their top wings, kept tight formation roughly three thousand feet below her. They were predators on the hunt for reconnaissance craft. Probably her, considering the sky they preoccupied. This must have meant Scarlett was over the Western Front. This was *her* sky.

Just stay on the mission directives, Hemsworth's voice echoed in her head. *Stick to that path and you will be back in France safe and sound.*

Get into Germany. Check.

Get the plans from Grandmother. Check, in a manner of speaking.

Get out. Check.

No heroics.

Yes, it was a very simple plan.

And yet there were five LVG's below her. They were looking for an old, antiquated Bristol Scout, held together by duty, honour, and sheer will.

Scarlett hit the "Acknowledgement" button on the alarm, then flipped the switches on her dash. Around her, she could feel a low thrum of power vibrate through her seat and tight cabin. One by one, the lights of offensive measures and defensive countermeasures switched from yellow to green. Scarlett's grip on the stick tightened as she sucked in a good amount of the frigid air then breathed out slowly, granting herself a small, heady rush.

Then she thrust the stick to the left, and began a quick descent on the patrol.

The front mounted guns of her Sopwith Hornet roared to life, and Scarlett followed with her eyes the trails of her white-hot tracer bullets as they blazed between her and the LVG's. She could just make out the enemy pilots frantically trying to see exactly where the hostile gunfire was coming from.

Two of the outer planes immediately broke formation while the lead plane and its right wingman both fell into Scarlett's sights. Their planes were devoured by fire and smoke as her bullets tore through the fuselage. With two kills in her opening manoeuvre, Scarlett brought the Hornet around in a wide, banking turn, and become quite lightheaded at the speed she was reaching. On coming out of the turn, she felt as if she had been thrown out of a slingshot, the velocity throwing her back in the seat but the Hornet remaining inconceivably stable.

The LVG in her sights bobbed left and right, trying to evade her bursts of incendiary bullets. Scarlett could have easily matched the tactics, but it would have also consumed more fuel, fuel she would need for both attack and evasion. She kept the Hornet steady, waiting for the LVG to slip back into her line of fire.

The Proximity Alarm screeched as a thought came to her: *I'm stationary up here. I'm a target.*

The Hornet twisted into a tight corkscrew just as bullets rained down from above her. Scarlett flipped the craft a fourth time, and then on the fifth roll she climbed up and then banked hard to see the descending LVG swoop past her and then try to pull out of its dive. Following her own turn, Scarlett felt the Hornet gain speed, close the gap between her and the enemy craft, and finally place the offending LVG square in her sights. With that plane out of the fight Scarlett banked hard in the opposite direction, turning to face the remaining two LVG's that had regrouped behind her. They were closing in fast, but she kept her own flightpath steady. She always did enjoy the gallant challenges Jerry would throw at her. They were curious as to what mettle she was made of, completely unaware this was the pilot they had often tangled with over the Western Front.

Let them guess. Scarlett was enjoying herself presently, feeling very much at home behind the controls of the Sopwith Hornet.

The LVG's broke off as Scarlett flew between them, the slipstream buffeting at her Hornet as she banked hard, countering their own attempts to get behind her. She could feel every snap of the rigging and flutter of canvas ripped open by bullet holes as her Hornet angrily buzzed across Belgian skies. The remaining LVG's parted, both of the enemy planes banking into opposite directions. She could easily line up a kill for one of them, but not without the other flanking her. There was always the option of pulling out of the fight, continuing home; but Scarlett wanted to finish what she had started.

Just stay on the mission directives. Stick to that path and you will be back in France safe and sound.

There was what she should do, and what she wanted to do.

Scarlett had the better machine, and now she needed to know if she had the skill to go with it. Her plane dipped left and then climbed up, its twin machine guns giving angry report to the LVG crossing into her gunsights. Her bullets angrily ripped into the plane's fuselage, tearing into the cockpit as she climbed. She didn't know the limits of this experimental, but she knew the climbing rate of the LVG. It was fast, but her Hornet's top speed might be a touch faster. She just had to stay ahead of her opponent, and at the best moment, get behind him. Tracer fire zipped by her cockpit and sparks flew from the Hornet's rigging. Old Jerry was not going to let her get away so quickly.

The Hornet, on Scarlett's biding, now dipped into a dive. Scarlett's intent would be to drop under her opponent, invert, then climb again. This experimental had shown itself capable of such a manoeuvre, but it all rested on the LVG not anticipating the tactic.

Scarlett threw her stick to the right, the horizon tumbled to where ground was sky, where up and down, and vice versa. Her plane pitched up, but her opponent was no longer there.

She looked left, then right, and the LVG had countered, banked, inverted, and levelled out to have Scarlett in the perfect kill shot.

The LVG disappeared in a brilliant explosion of fire, smoke, and a storm of tracer bullets from above her. What should have been the plane that plucked her from the skies now plummeted to the earth thousands of feet below her.

For the first time, she saw the Proximity Alarm's light display turn red. This device was not designed to know friend from foe, just let the pilot know that another plane was far-too-close-for-comfort. So whomever rescued Scarlett from the LVG was getting cosy at ten thousand feet in the air.

Something swooped from above and came so close to her right that their wingtips were nearly touching. Scarlett felt her grip tighten on the Hornet's stick as the black Fokker tri-wing fighter plane silently few alongside her. The pilot looked over to her and saluted.

Scarlett recognized that dark gaze instantly. It was the same gaze that had held her own in Grandmother's house. She had punched Maximiliane Adolphina Vogelberg von Wolff. She had punched the Big Bad Wolf.

And now, the Big Bad Wolf had just rescued her from certain death?

No, Scarlett thought as the Ace of Aces gave her a nod before pulling away, *Wolff wanted the kill.* She was not going to let anyone else have it, nor let anyone stand in her way.

The Big Bad Wolf zipped ahead of Scarlett, placing the silent aircraft in front of her gunsights. She was not certain of what this tactic was all about, but neither would she question it. Scarlett pulled the trigger of her twin machine guns but the triplane pitched up almost at a perfect vertical angle, inverted itself, and then levelled out behind her. She banked the Hornet hard to the left, while easing up on the throttle, giving Wolff plenty of time and space to overshoot and get ahead of her.

What Wolff made her plane do should have been impossible, should have torn the plane apart; but the triple-winged plane appeared to spin on its horizontal, as if it were simply skating across a frozen pond, and opened fire as she glided past. Bullets struck something on the Hornet, and on Scarlett's "Damage Control" dashboard, the tail section lit up.

She had taken damage, but the display could not tell exactly what kind. What Scarlett could take certainty in was any violent manoeuvres could result in a rigging failure and a loss of control in her rudder.

No doubt Wolff also knew this.

Time to leave.

Scarlett pulled back on the stick, opening the throttle. She could feel the cold air biting at her skin, the speed of her Sopwith Hornet pushing her back into her seat once more. She had cleared the Proximity Alert, and so far her own escape appeared uninterrupted. Even with a green light from the alarm, Scarlett scanned the skies for any sign of Wolff. The Fokker prototype was nowhere below her nor to any other side.

Then she looked up, and at her six she caught a glimpse of the three-winged silhouette.

Her eyes switched back to the "Damage Control" display. Her usual manoeuvres of corkscrews and hard dives would have to be a last resort, if at all.

Plus, she had tricks of her own.

Scarlett thrust the stick to her right, turning the plane on its side as Wolff continued to dive on her, the rain of bullets missing her by a few feet. The Fokker buzzed past and then suspended itself, just as it had with that horizontal spin, and then propelled itself upwards, now closing in from behind.

"Let's try this option," Scarlett muttered, flipping the countermeasure switch that read "Flares."

Just over her cockpit's windshield, there was a small mirror that allowed for her to see the tail section of her Hornet. The small calibre turret, its barrel no bigger than a hand pistol, rapidly launched bright balls of blue flame. They hurtled towards the Schwarzer Geist, but then exploded mere feet before the propellers.

Scarlett tore her eyes away from the sudden flashes that flared from her rear-view mirror, and pulled back hard on the stick, taking her Hornet up and over. Once inverted, she looked up to see the black Fokker pass underneath her. Wolff was bobbing and weaving in some sort of evasion tactic.

Scarlett continued the loop, her attention now on the "Damage Control" panel that showed the lights on the tail section blinking between yellow and red, settling thankfully on yellow once she slipped behind Wolff.

"Fine," she said through clenched teeth, "let's end this."

She pulled the trigger, peppering the plane in front of her with bullets; but only for a few seconds before a new light flickered brightly on her dashboard: *Ammunition Low.*

The Fokker tumbled out of sight, but this was not the death spiral all pilots recognized. This was a controlled descent. Scarlett could not run out of ammunition while over the Front. She had to make it to the border, return to French skies. She was so close.

Then it came to her. She really could be thick at times.

Tracer fire zipped by her cockpit and between the struts of her Hornet. If she were going to make for her escape, it had to be now.

Scarlett flipped the Hornet's motor from "Patrol" to "Combat/Evasion" mode. The engine rumbled to an eerie silence, but her plane launched itself into the horizon, the lightest of touches from Scarlett on the stick sending the plane into wild corkscrews. She was now in full electric mode, and miles ahead of Wolff.

On her dashboard, the map of the Western Front scrolled by at a consistent, steady pace, far faster than she had ever seen. The speedometer only measured as high as one hundred fifty miles per hour, but the needle inched beyond that before it stopped, unable to go any further.

The Proximity Alarm screeched. Scarlett looked in her rear-view and could see in the distance the outline of the Fokker prototype. The Big Bad Wolf had let her go once, most likely out of a sense of chivalry. They had been mismatched. Now, the rules of combat were at play. Wolff was not intending on repeating the gesture to Scarlett. Not after Grandmother's house.

Her gaze jumped back to the map. The French border was far behind her. Rang-du-Fliers was closing in fast.

So was the Schwarzer Geist.

Scarlett pushed forward on the stick, taking her Hornet into a long, slow dive. She would have to try and shake off Wolff, if fuel and luck would have it, somewhere over the English Channel. Whatever the cost, she could not afford to reveal her hidden airfield.

The order suddenly lit up on her dash. This was a new communications system that both Tink and Hemsworth both cooked up, produced, and managed to fix into the dashboard before she left for Germany. With the late afternoon sun now beginning a descent before her and Wolff still within a warning distance, the message painted on its long, slender glass plate seemed to burn insistently.

Return to Base.

Someone must have sighted them at the Front, relayed a message back to Rang-du-Fliers. Still, this message was sent? Were they serious?

Her eyes went to the fuel and battery gauge. The battery was close to dry. The fuel would be enough to get her to base, but only just. If she were to try for Calais, it would mean a death at sea for both of them.

"You had better be right about this, Adams," she swore as the Hornet levelled out and headed for home.

Scarlett flipped the engine mode back to "Patrol" which, in turn, brought the petrol engine back online. The changeover was instantaneous as the Hornet's fuselage shuddered. Scarlett also lost the incredible response time in her controls. There may be a few miles left on the battery, a sudden kick which she might need once over the airfield.

The forest underneath her whizzed by and then disappeared, just as the Proximity Alarm went red. Scarlett's gaze went back to the rear-view. Wolff would be within the perfect firing range in seconds.

The explosion to her left caused her to pull up instinctively, but then she realized the low-ceiling flack was not for her. Around Wolff, shells exploded, dotting the sky with dark patches of black. Scarlett looked down, and beat the side of the Hornet's fuselage as she cheered madly. On either side of her landing strip were three massive, all-terrain "Lions." Their back legs were in a crouch position while the front legs were straightened to their full length. With the extra angle, Hemsworth's tanks could now take aim on the incoming Fokker.

One shell ripped through two of her right wings, but the airplane continued its pursuit, opening fire on the Hornet.

This time the bullet cut through the fuselage, and searing pain swept over Scarlett's shoulder.

No, Scarlett, she chided herself, *that's an insane thought.*

Insane, but perhaps her best option at present.

She flipped the Hornet back into "Combat/Evasion" mode, and within seconds the electric motor took control. Scarlett then threw the plane into a wild corkscrew, hoping Wolff would follow. Then on her third loop, Scarlett pulled back on the stick hard while angling flaps as hard as they could go. She felt the Hornet turn in such a way, she could not be certain of her control over the plane. Around her, everything blurred by as if she were on a merry-go-round moving too fast, and what was behind her was in front of her.

Scarlett pulled trigger, emptying her twin machine guns into the Big Bad Wolf.

The plane now hurtled at her in a great ball of fire. Scarlett jerked back hard on the stick and her wheels bumped against the top wing of the Fokker.

The petrol engine gurgled back to life, and for a moment Scarlett fought to keep the Hornet flying as nothing was responding straight away. Yellow and red lights blinked madly across her dashboard. It was impossible in this eternal second of time to tell if she were flying or falling gracefully from the sky, but the pain in her shoulder offered her flashes of alertness.

The throttle was not cut back. The Hornet was levelling out. The runway was no longer a moving target. This time, Scarlett's landing only included a bounce five feet high before the plane rolled to a stop.

Scarlett slumped back into her seat as she stubbornly tried to power down the plane before passing out. "I must be getting better at the landing," was last thing she remembered hearing herself say before surrendering to the darkness.

SIX

o, why are we here again?" asked Hemsworth.

"Perspective," Scarlett replied, holding the glass just shy of her lips before saying again, "perspective."

Before the tank commander and the pilot, the English Channel ebbed and flowed. At least they knew it did. From where they looked over Calais, there were no waves to follow with their eyes. Simply a blue canvas stretching for miles. As it was a particularly clear day, they could see the faint outline of England on the horizon. For King, Country, and the Empire.

But was it all worth it?

Now Scarlett completely understood why Tink came up here. Alone with thoughts. A moment's reflection here, in private.

Her gaze wandered over to the broad-shouldered soldier, enjoying the afternoon with her atop this particular outlook. "How much longer, you think?"

"Oh, a few more days, then I should probably contact H.Q. and tell them I will be back on the front with a new pride of Lions."

Scarlett laughed. "No, silly, I meant with the war. The Great War. How much longer, you think?"

Hemsworth ran his fingers through his blonde hair, letting out a long, slow breath. He seemed to hold his breath a lot around her. He really needed to just relax a bit, enjoy life. "It would have been shorter had you not retrieved the plans of the Schwarzer Geist, but it would also have been a different world under the Kaiser."

"Makes me wonder then if it was worth it."

"Now hold on, Little Red, you can't look at it that way."

Scarlett raised an eyebrow. "Oh, really? And exactly how am I supposed to look at it, Major?"

He leaned back into the grass, propping himself up on his elbows. "Perhaps that come out wrong."

"I invited you up here so I could share this experience with you, as a way to say thank you. Don't make me regret this."

"What I meant was, you are helping to find a balance with the way the world works. One of the reasons why war happens usually comes down to what one side has and the other doesn't. When you think about it, that explains what's happening right now."

Scarlett chuckled. "You make it sound like the Great War is really a group of spoiled children fighting over the same toy."

"Maybe," he said, finishing off his glass of wine. "I just know if you hadn't taken the chance, hadn't risked your life for King and Country, right now the Kaiser would have a weapon in their arsenal we wouldn't know how to combat."

"The Hornet did just fine."

"Yes, but the Fokker was different. You saw it up close. Hopefully, we can replicate from those schematics how they solved the range and temperature problem of the engine."

"And how does that help the war effort again?"

"Well…" Hemsworth began, but his thought seemed to falter. Finally, he said, "We were able to stop a dangerous weapon from being potentially exclusive to the enemy."

"Did it ever occur to you that in a war, there is no hero and villain, no noble knight and mortal enemy? In our Great War, we see Germany as the enemy out to crush us under their boot heel, while Germany sees us as the overbearing Empire forcing our unwanted policies and restrictions on their way of life which was fine…until we can along and told them 'No, do it this way.' Being Irish, I can understand how that feels."

Hemsworth went to speak, but again, took a long moment before finally replying, "Is this the perspective you wanted to share with me up here?"

"Actually, no, I just wanted to share a bottle of fine wine with you and I really can't do it all by myself at present," she said, motioning to the one arm in a sling.

"How is the shoulder healing up?"

"Should be back up in the skies in no time," she said cheerily. "That being said, pour me another glass."

"I'll have to get the other basket," he said, returning to his feet.

She watched as Hemsworth trotted over to the massive Lion and retrieved from behind the "paw" closest to him another basket with a bottle of wine and two freshly baked loaves of bread.

"Did I ever thank you for coming to my rescue, Major Hemsworth?" she asked, holding up her glass.

The cork slipped out with a short, crisp *pop*. He passed the open bottle under his nose and smiled appreciatively. "Actually, no you didn't, Captain Quinn," he said, pouring her glass, "and what with rushing you to a hospital, the promotion, and debriefing, I don't think we got around to it. But if you want to thank me, try this on for size…" Hemsworth poured himself a new glass, and then held it up into the breeze. "Harry."

Scarlett tipped her head to one side. "Sorry?"

"Harry. Please. Call me Harry."

She looked him over from head-to-toe, then shook her head. "No, I prefer Hemsworth. Seems to suit you better. What with those broad shoulders, blond hair, and blue eyes, you don't look like a Harry."

His mouth turned into a slight scowl. "I'm not really enjoying this perspective, Little Red, you know that?"

Her eyes narrowed on him. "You know I'm not particularly keen on that nickname."

"Your choice," he said with a shrug. "Call me Harry, and we can drop this whole nickname nonsense."

Scarlett puckered her lips, took a moment to look out over the Channel, then took a sip of her wine. "Thanks, Hemsworth, for being there. I don't know if I couldn't have done it without you."

Harry took a seat next to her, and gently nudged her. "You were the one who shot down the Big Bad Wolf. You were fine. I just made a promise to you I would offer support. I did, as I said I would, and I would do it again. But as for the thought, think nothing of it," and he touched his glass with hers, "Little Red."

photo by Bruce F. Press

New Zealand-born fantasy writer and podcaster **Philippa (Pip) Ballantine** is the author of the *Books of the Order* series, and has appeared in collections such as *Steampunk World* and *Clockwork Fairy Tales*. She is also the co-author with her husband, **Tee Morris,** of *Social Media for Writers*. Tee co-authored *Podcasting for Dummies* and has contributed articles and stories for numerous anthologies including *Farscape Forever!, Tales of a Tesla Ranger,* and *A Cosmic Christmas 2 You.*

Together, they are the creators of the Ministry of Peculiar Occurrences. Both the series and its companion podcast, *Tales from the Archives,* have won numerous awards including the 2011 Airship Award for Best in Steampunk Literature, the 2013 Parsec Award for Best Podcast Anthology, and RT Reviewers' Choice for Best Steampunk of 2014. Their latest title, *The Curse of the Silver Pharaoh,* debuted at #1 under three different Steampunk categories on Amazon.com.

The two reside in Manassas, Virginia with their daughter and a mighty clowder of cats. You can find out more about them and explore more of the Ministry at **ministryofpeculiaroccurrences.com**

Made in the USA
San Bernardino, CA
28 March 2017